FRIEND

OF ACPL

CO. SCHOOLS

Sam Bottleby

Sam Bottleby

RUTH CHRISTOFFER CARLSEN

Illustrated by Wallace Tripp

1968 HOUGHTON MIFFLIN COMPANY BOSTON

Other Books by
RUTH CHRISTOFFER CARLSEN

Mr. Pudgins
Henrietta Goes West
Hildy and the Cuckoo Clock
Monty and the Tree House

COPYRIGHT © 1968 BY RUTH CHRISTOFFER CARLSEN
ALL RIGHTS RESERVED INCLUDING THE RIGHT
TO REPRODUCE THIS BOOK OR PARTS THEREOF IN ANY FORM
LIBRARY OF CONGRESS CATALOG CARD NUMBER: 68-29898
PRINTED IN THE U. S. A.

For CARL and LYDIA CHRISTOFFER,
my father and mother.
Like Sam they enjoyed both gadgets
and the unexpected.

ED. SCHOOLS
C711594

CONTENTS

1

A First-Class Adventure?

Well, we'd made it. We had actually arrived at Kennedy Airport in New York as planned. But what a mess! No parents. They were still in Paris waiting for their plane to be repaired. Some mechanical difficulty. So instead of a gala welcome and a big tour of New York and Washington, we were faced by this airline official looking as if he'd just swallowed a mouthful of lemons. Course, he had good reason for his expression, that's certain sure. The airline mechanics were threatening to strike at midnight and this Uniform was scared to death he was going to have a couple of kids on his hands indefinitely. I looked down at Solveig — she's my bratty sister. About knee-high to a grasshopper, long dark hair, violet eyes, and no words. She'd been in an auto accident when she was three and hardly said a word since. Big comfort she was. And me? I'm Trygve Samsen, just turned twelve and definitely in trouble. But that's nothing new.

"You children go sit over there. I'm sending you back to St. Paul on the four o'clock flight."

My heart went *plonk,* because my Dad had told us to meet him in New York City. And my Dad expected strict obedience to his orders. I felt caught in a trap. Looked to me as if I was going to be in trouble no matter what I did. "Come on, kid. Get moving," said the Uniform.

I don't know where the words came from. But they did. "Pardon me, sir, but Solveig wants to go to the Ladies' Room. Will that be all right?"

The Uniform's face twisted kind of angry-like. I guess he was the kind that didn't like his plans upset. Tough bounce for him! Because I intended to upset his plans plenty. Solveig and I simply had to get away. With a little luck I knew we could. I only half listened to the directions to the Ladies' Room. But I started out in the direction the Uniform indicated as if we were really going there. Only the Uniform wouldn't give up. He stood there shouting more instructions after me. "By the way, son, pick up your luggage on the way back here. I'll toss the key to you. Locker 709. Got it?"

I got it all right, though I had to scramble to catch the key. And we started off again, Solveig clutching her dirty panda bear against her stomach. But right then I hit a problem. Solveig might not talk, but she wasn't deaf. And she'd heard me mention the Ladies' Room. So darned if she didn't make me take her there. Have you ever waited outside one of those places? Because with Solveig I could count on a long wait. She had this thing about soap dispensers. She loved experimenting with them. Sounds crazy? Well, that was Solveig. I knew any stop-off in a Ladies' Room by my kid sister could take time — lots of time. I began to panic, pacing up and down that long, hard floor — waiting, waiting, waiting. How could we escape — yes, escape — run away — if she didn't step on it?

And then, there she was, looking lost and sad and miserable. She had nothing on me. I was feeling the same things myself. But I grabbed her hand, cleanest hand in town I bet, and I absolutely ran her toward the outside door. I could hear them calling our names over the loudspeaker. They were paging us. It's scary to hear your name bounding and bopping off walls. We got through the doors and I really shoved her into the first bus, a white and gold thing waiting at the curb. Lucky for me it was the bus that shuttled between the different buildings at Kennedy. Why, that place is a regular village in itself. Course the ride cost money. Twenty-five cents for each of us. And that scared me some, because I didn't have a big stock of money on hand. But I paid. We were just pulling away from the curb when the Uniform rushed out looking this way and that. But he didn't see us.

So what happened those next hours? Nothing. And nothing takes longer to happen than anything I know. We got off at the International Arrival Building, which was a good choice because half of New York must have been right there trying to get flights before the

midnight deadline. It was a madhouse. And in a mad-house who notices two kids.

First I dragged Solveig in to eat. Then we spent hours watching planes come and go. And I played counting games and color games and surely-Mom-and-Dad-will-be-on-the-next-plane games and slowly the clock's hands moved toward midnight. That was about as far as I could think. The mechanics were supposed to strike at midnight. And if they did, then maybe Solveig and I would be allowed to wait for the folks somewhere in New York City. I hadn't figured out how the folks could get to New York if there were a strike. You have to take one problem at a time, I figure.

I tried drinking coffee to stay awake. Solveig simply gave up and went to sleep smack on the floor, her head on her Daffy bear. And finally it happened. The hands on the clock reached twelve — ten after twelve — twelve-thirty. The last planes must have left for St. Paul. I was pretty sure of that. So I dragged Solveig to her feet and we took the bus back to the terminal to pick up our bags. I remembered that they were stashed in locker 709. So what happens? A treasure hunt. I've never seen so many rows of lockers in my life. And they tuck them in all over the place. When you're really beat, a hunt like that is no fun. It's horrible. But to make things worse, when I finally found the right number, I couldn't find the key. I went through my billfold. I felt in my pockets. And Solveig helped me out full volume. She folded up on the floor and started to wail and bellow. Her sounds were enough to raise the dead. And she raised something all right.

Because smack in my ear something went, "Tut . . . tut . . . tut."

What a weird sound. Have you ever been tut-tutted? It's enough to give each corpuscle a private goose bump. I began to shake and I didn't know if I was only tired or plain scared to death. So I looked behind me. Galloping guppies! The sounds had come from a man. I think it was a man. I say that because he wasn't any taller than me and I'm considered short for my age. We stood there, sort of eye to eye with Solveig's yowling absolutely blotting out thought.

This short guy had black, snappy eyes and red hair. Mine is kind of carrot-colored but his was a red that had to have come from a bottle. It was that violent. Only it wasn't in the usual places. He had a fringe of it all around the top, a scrub brush of it bulging over his eyebrows and a small pointy beard. And then he had this nose, a very squashy-type nose with a very red, very prominent bump smack at the end. I think I've heard it called a wen.

"Stop that noise this minute," said the character. He

"You are wrong there," he said. "I am your godfather." I could see there was no point arguing. But I couldn't help trying.

"But Mr. Bottleby, sir . . ."

"Call me Sam," said the strange one.

I started again. "Well, Sam, it isn't possible."

"Nonsense. I guess I know what is possible." And suddenly his eyes looked mighty fierce. I shut up. "Your name," said Sam Bottleby, "is Samsen. That is right?"

Even Solveig sort of nodded agreement.

"And I get all the Sam's as godchildren. Quite obvious, it would seem."

It didn't seem very obvious to me. But Solveig got to her feet, came over. And she spoke. I couldn't believe my ears. Solveig was saying one word after another, just like most people. Only I wished she hadn't. Her words were so dumb. "Are you . . ." she stopped. "Are you a . . . a . . . fairy godfather?" she asked.

"FAIRY GODFATHER." Those words exploded out of me.

Oh, boy, I was so embarrassed I couldn't look at Sam Bottleby. Kid sisters can be awful pains. But you know what he said? He said, "Of course. I thought you'd know."

My mouth fell open and I stared. I was tired, you see, and I began to have very peculiar thoughts — like was I awake or asleep? You just don't meet fairy godfathers in airports. Especially big New York City airports. But Solveig promptly put her hand in his and smiled very smugly to herself. And without even looking at me, they started off. "Hey, the bags, the bags," I called after them.

Sam looked back at me. Then he looked at the bags. And frit-frat, he did a funny thing. He rubbed that red bump on his nose with his thumb, looking very thoughtful as he did it. And gently those bags floated up into the air and followed along behind Sal and that dwarf of a Sam as they moved away from me. I heard somebody snicker. Somebody else said, "How are they doing that?"

I could feel my face turning red. How embarrassing to be with a freak who did such wild things. I ran after them, quick as quick, grabbed the handles of the bags, and was going to pretend I was carrying them. Only it didn't work out that way. I got carried by the bags. I couldn't seem to get my feet down to the floor.

I heard Solveig saying, "Are all fairy godfathers small like you?"

"Small?" Sam stopped so suddenly that I gave him a nudge from behind. "Aha!" he said. "I wondered why everyone stared. I am too small?"

"You can say that again," I said. "You're dwarf size, Sam. It's all right," I hastened to add. Because maybe that's the size fairy godfathers came in. I hadn't had much experience with them.

"Botheration and bubble gum!" said Sam. "It's these newfangled formulas. They've gone very modern in my land, you know. Everything is formulas now." It sort of shook me up when I realized that Sam must be referring to fairyland. "Let's see, I'll have to try for a little more size."

So right then and there, while we're standing there, watching, but mainly wondering, he started in on this business of rubbing the bump on his nose. Suddenly he and I weren't seeing eye to eye. Because Sam was stretching out above me — growing up and up. "Watch it, Sam!" I sort of snorted. "Watch it — your clothes . . ."

I had this mad picture of Sam bursting out of his clothes which would be mighty embarrassing and would surely land us in more trouble.

"Don't worry, boy," said Sam, still growing. "We're very modern, I told you. Stretch clothes are all the rage in my homeland. Is this a better size?"

"Hey, wait. Hold it." I didn't know quite what words to use to tell him to stop growing. It was something I'd never had to do before. But Sam had stopped rubbing his wen. The only way I can describe his size is to say he was towering over us. He had been strange-looking with his red fringe of hair and pointed beard in the economy size, but he was overwhelming at six feet four. It all made me feel a little strange. What were we in to?

Only I didn't have long to think about this because Sam was telling me I had to send a telegram to my folks and let them know that all was well. Before I knew it I was writing out a cablegram. That was simple enough. But the paying for it was a problem.

Seems in a cable they make you pay for every word. Even the numbers in the address. I asked Sam if he minded paying. He said, "No, not at all." Only he went on to explain that he couldn't because they didn't use money where he came from. I got the queer shivers again. Could this be a con game, with me paying all the way. But I was too tired to worry. That takes energy. So I did the next best thing and cut out words, lots of words, from the cable. It finally read, "Safe. Sam here. Trygve."

Much later I learned that it had gotten messed up. "Save Sam here." What was meant to be reassuring turned out to be confusing. To my folks, I mean.

After I got the change back, I turned toward Sam and listen, he was staring at all those madly jiggling sending machines and typewriters like a bear looks at honey. "Hey, Sam, what now?"

Sam jerked, as if I'd waked him up from a dream. "Marvelous gadgets, those," he said. "People persons have such ingenuity. How I'd love to get my hands on them. All of them."

I felt a little twinge of fright. And then I felt nothing but an overpowering desire to go to sleep. Right then. Sam must have seen how things were with us. Because he said, "Come, Trig. Time you and Sal got to bed."

"Her name is not Sal, it's Solveig," I said it very slowly. I couldn't even make my words move fast. "And my name is Trygve."

"Nonsense. Your names are Trig and Sal. Let's get

a cab." And just like that he whistled to the bags and started off with the luggage floating behind him like two well-trained dogs. Solveig had hold of his hand. I had to trot to keep up. "My folks don't like nicknames. We are Solveig and Trygve." It's awfully hard talking convincingly to a pair of backs. "Besides, Trig sounds like a horse," I muttered.

Sam stopped. Solveig stopped. The bags stopped. And I staggered on by. My brain never signaled a stop. Sam's hand reached out and grabbed me. I stopped. "Nicknames are love names," he said firmly. "If you think Trig is too horsey, then think of it in your mind as spelled Tryg. And this little thing," he nodded at my sister, "is too young for such a ponderous name as Solveig. Her name is Sal. Now let's go."

And they did. I grabbed the handles on the bags because with their floating power I could just drift with no work at all. Down the escalators we went, out the doors, and into the first taxi. We sat there waiting. The taxi driver turned around and said in a sour voice, "Those bags yours, mister?"

"Botheration," said Sam. "Almost forgot them."

And while he was saying this he was rubbing the bump. Next thing, the front door of the cab opened. The bags floated in and settled on the seat. The door closed. The taxi driver sat there looking, first at the bags, then back at us, then at the bags. "Man and boy," he said, "I've been driving in New York now

some twenty years. And I ain't seen the like of that. You some kind of a performer?" he asked Sam.

"Something like that," said Sam. I snickered. "Take us to the New York Manor House."

"Hey, Sam . . ." I was going to ask about the cost, because if they had no money in Sam's land then I could pretty well figure out who was going to be doing the paying — me. Now I could maybe handle the bills at a Y.M.C.A. — but the Manor House? Ouch! Only I didn't get the question out because somebody else was asking questions. A policeman. He had stuck his head through the open window. "Hey, you. These kids with you?"

Man, he was looking at Sam fiercely. My heart began doing this mad rat-a-tat-tat. And Solveig — I mean Sal — she looked terrified. But Sam was very calm. "Certainly, Officer, these children are with me." You'd have thought he was a judge, the way he rolled those words out. "These are my godchildren, sir. Drive on, Cabby."

The policeman looked apologetic. "Sorry, sir. I'm a little jumpy. Two kids disappeared this afternoon. Vanished. Could be bad."

"Could be," said Sam. "On the other hand, it could be nothing at all."

And with that the cab started moving. What a relief. I leaned back against the seat, struggling to keep my eyes open. Which was a little difficult since my eyelids seemed weighted with concrete. My brain was buzzing with funny little fragments of thoughts. You know how it is when you're dozing off. Thoughts like, who is this Sam? Is he really a con man? An actor? A magic person? I didn't linger on that last thought. It was too wild. So I bounced off to wondering about the folks and the airline strike and then I thought about money. Where could I find money for a stay in New York? Aw, heck! I was too tired to think about money.

Right about then I realized Sam was talking — to me I think. He said something like, "I always say, if you're going to have an adventure, make it a first-class one. And for heaven's sakes — plunge in and enjoy it." I thought he had stopped, but he hadn't. "Don't worry about money, Tryg. Something will turn up. Something always does."

I wanted to say that what might turn up was the police. But I didn't. Instead I fell asleep thinking that now I not only had my stupid little sister to look after but also some kind of a wacky nut who called himself our godfather.

2

Up, Up and Away

Sᴀᴍ ʜᴀᴅ ɴᴏ ᴘʀᴏʙʟᴇᴍ in getting us a room at the Manor House. The size he had grown to was so impressive that the room clerk looked like a dwarf by comparison. And then there were his clothes. He had on a bright yellow vest, tweedy green coat, and these strange-looking boots with deep cuffs at the top. But it was the trousers that were most surprising. They were so tight-fitting that you marveled how Sam could get all of him inside the material. Was he copying the olden days or something in the future? Anyway, he was the kind of individual that people turn to stare at. Being slightly bashful myself, I felt embarrassed at all the stares and tried to fade into the woodwork. Not easy to do with carrot-colored hair and a million freckles.

Why the bell captain insisted on carrying up our two bags to the room, I don't know. I certainly could have handled them myself. But he did. He led us toward the banks of elevators. There were so many floors in this hotel that they had rows of elevators and each row stopped at a different set of floors. The set we took stopped at the floors numbered 32 to 45. Zoom! We flashed up non-stop those first 32 floors which made my stomach sink right into my shoes. That's how fast we were moving. Then I noticed Sam. He was staring at the panel of buttons the way I look at a double fudge sundae. It was sure a happy look and yet it kind of scared me too. "This is your floor," said the bell captain and stepped aside to let us out of the elevator.

Sam came to with a start. "Marvelous gadgets, these elevators. Marvelous."

He said this to no one in particular. Made me feel funny. Who was Sam, really? I mean what kind of person thinks of elevators as gadgets? I might have argued the point with Sam except right then he saw that Solveig, oops, Sal, was sound asleep. She had slipped all the way down to the floor, her back against the wall, her head nodding almost down to her lap. Sam swept her up in his arms and strode off after the bell captain. Once at the room, Sam dumped Sal on one of the beds, turned to me and said, "Tip the boy, Tryg."

I felt in my pockets for change. Darn it. I didn't have anything smaller than a twenty-five-cent piece. So I handed the man this. I don't know why he acted so mad. If I'd had something smaller I'd have given it to him. I considered him lucky, myself.

I don't remember getting undressed and into pajamas. But I must have. I had them on in the morning. I also had a sort of blurred memory of a maid bringing in a rollaway bed which Sam promptly mussed up after she had left. And then he said something about ordering the rollaway because the clerk might have wondered at three people in a room with only two beds. After that he muttered that he was off to his own land to handle some unfinished business. He rubbed his bump and said some strange-sounding words and between the moment he raised his hand to switch out the lights and the moment the room went dark, Sam disappeared. And so did I. Right into sleep.

Man! What wonderful smells I awoke to the next morning. Bacon and pancakes and toast and fresh strawberries. Which is an impossible blend of smells to be having on the fortieth floor of a New York hotel.

Only it wasn't impossible. Because smack between Sal and my beds was this little table on wheels. There were all sorts of platters with silver covers and bowls of this and that. I whipped off the cover quick-like and found French toast all puffed up, with maple syrup in one pitcher and red raspberry syrup in another just waiting to go on. Bacon and toast and a puffy egg thing like I'd never seen before was under another cover. And there were stacks of teensy pancakes with blueberry sauce dripping off them under another. And waffles and toast and Post Toasties with strawberries and thick cream. I can't even name all that Sam had either ordered or dreamed up. I didn't know which. But it was a feast, like no breakfast I'd

ever had before. Sal and I fell on that food as if we
were starving. Which we were, I guess.

Sam was there all right. In a big armchair near the
window. Only I didn't really look at him, because I
was so busy eating. And when I did look at him, I
stopped eating. Because he was a sight. If he had
looked like a dwarf last night, he looked like a walking
doll today. He sat there, swinging his feet off the floor
because obviously he couldn't get them down to the
floor.

"Ahem," I said, because I was talking around a big
hunk of pancake. Sam looked my way. He could tell
I was trying to say something. But he couldn't tell
what. I swallowed the chunk of food whole and it
glunked its way down to my stomach. "You're too
small, Sam," I said. "Last night you were small, but
today you're ridiculous."

"Botheration," said Sam, snapping his fingers excitedly. "So that's why the waiter acted so oddly. He
actually backed out the door, staring as he went."

I could understand that. Sam was something to rate
stares. "Back to the formula," said Sam. "But I do
wish people persons were a little more adaptable to
change. They think in such rigid ways." Knowing
how adults react I could understand Sam's remarks.
Well, Sam rubbed his bump and muttered under his
breath and began to grow. Not in the grand sweeping
upness of last night, but in little jerky, bouncy spurts.
I even stopped eating to watch. If you think it's fun

to see a plant go upward, you should try watching a person growing, right before your eyes. Beats television.

"That's enough, Sam," I said.

Sam stopped his growing and I went back to my eating. But not for long. Because I'd reached that point where I thought I might burst if I kept on stuffing more food in. I put the napkin back on the table with a satisfied sigh. And next thing I knew, Sal and I were getting showered and into clean clothes and ready for something. I didn't know what. Of course, Sal couldn't make up her mind right off whether she should wear the white shirt with red shorts or red shirt with white shorts or neither. Oh boy! Girls. But finally the great decision was made. She settled for her red shorts, white T-shirt and bright red tennis shoes. What with Sam's red hair and pointy beard, my own carrot-colored stuff, and Sal's outfit, we really covered the possibilities in red.

Sam kind of steered us toward the elevators. And the maid was standing in the hall, staring at us like we were freaks. Mostly she was looking at Sam. She said something, kind of under her breath as I passed. It sounded like, "That Fred needs his eyes examined. Shure and begorra, I told him the man in four-o-o-seven was a tall one. And him saying he was a dwarf. P'fft." The sound started me snickering. Sam was certainly keeping the help confused. Nothing rigid about Sam, I'd say.

The elevator arrived at our floor and Sam ushered us

in. Down we plummeted. It felt like we were falling smack to the bottom of the shaft and then some. I heard this funny gasp from behind me. I suppose it was Sal. At the bottom, as we were bouncing to a stop, Sal said, "Let's do that again, Sam."

And just like that, we did do it again. Talk about speed. I was glued to the floor by pressure. It sure felt as if we were going to be airborne. At the forty-fifth floor we bounced and bounced, recovering from the stop. Then whoosh! Down we zoomed. Then up, then down, then up. My stomach was so excited it didn't know whether to zip out at my throat or my heels. And my heartbeat was keeping pace with our speed. That Sam, he was having such fun that it looked as if we might be going up and down, up and down for the rest of the morning.

But suddenly we got a change in routine. The light over the door registered the main floor. Zap! The doors flew open. And a man and woman stepped in. Now Sam was big but this fellow was even bigger. He was wearing boots too and the biggest cowboy hat I'd ever seen. He didn't even take it off. And the woman? She was something. Tiny, plump, teetering on spike heels and wearing a hat that was all pink feathers. But it was her purse that was startling. It was a large alligator thing, so large you wondered how she could manage all the weight. And she was talking. She was talking when she got on and she kept right on talking.

The man said, "Forty-fifth floor." He didn't even say please. Guess he thought Sam was the elevator operator. And whenever the woman paused for breath, the man would say, kind of automatically, "Yes, Birdie," or "No, Birdie."

It was a strange name, but it fit. We got to the forty-fifth floor in no time flat, but even the speed didn't slow down that woman's talking. I bet she even speeded up to keep in time with the elevator. The light over the door flashed 45. But the doors stayed shut. We bounced madly for a moment and the woman almost fell down. Spike heels are a little tee-tery for bouncing. Then zoom! We were off down-ward. That woman was little, but she made up for size in volume. Listen, she was shrieking so that my ears were pinned back by sheer sound. She was shrieking at both her husband and Sam to do some-thing. And her husband just stood there with a very blank look. Hey, I think he had tuned her out. Be-cause he said again, "Yes, Birdie."

Which started Birdie into a screaming tirade about men, machines, and elevators in particular. The light flashed 1. We bounced to a stop on the main floor. And started up at the double. She screeched, "We'll be killed. We'll be killed." And then she ran out of breath or something because she only made little moaning sounds. And big old Mr. Cowboy stood there blank-like, not registering a thing.

Of course, the idea of getting killed was absolutely ridiculous. After all, we'd been riding this same ele-vator for at least half an hour and we certainly weren't dead. We might have kept on like that forever — Sam

smiling in a happy fashion and punching buttons, Sal
and me grinning like zombies on a roller coaster ride,
Birdie moaning and Mr. Cowboy thinking his own
thoughts if Solveig — there I go again, I mean Sal —
hadn't opened her mouth. I was so used to Sal being
absolutely silent that it shook me up when she spoke.
But what she said shook me even more. "Oh, Sam,"
she said. "It feels like flying. I wish we were flying."

"First class," said Sam. "Why not?" At which moment I got these crazy chills across the back of my

neck, because frit-frat, Sam was rubbing that bump on his nose.

Birdie suddenly stopped moaning and ordered Sam to stop the elevator. She must have noticed the light flash *45*. The elevator didn't stop. It kept going up. And the numbers kept changing and going up in size. Just after *57* flashed by we felt a peculiar jar and jerk and heard strange tearing sounds as if something was ripping apart. Then there was absolute silence. No motor sounds at all. Even Birdie was silent. You might describe her as frozen. It was really fascinating to watch the numbers roll by. Numbers like *110, 111, 112*. Because you see, the Manor House had only fifty-seven floors.

It felt as if we were picking up speed because the numbers were going by so fast they were hard to read. I could feel the pressure of the speed. It felt as if someone had put a big concrete block on my head and was slowly grinding me into the floor. I think Sal had her wish all right. We were airborne, zooming off into upper air in an elevator. I snorted at the thought. Whoever heard of a flying elevator?

I don't know what there is about numbers changing fast like that. But it sure had us hypnotized. We all stood watching. Nobody speaking. The numbers got up to *3000*, then *3450*. I was beginning to feel scared all over again. I guess Birdie must have had identical feelings. Because she went into action. After so much silence it was surprising. But even more surprising, because I myself was beginning to feel sleepy and very lazy. Altitude, I guess. Sam didn't look too alert himself. He was reaching toward the panel of buttons and almost had his hand on the one marked *EMER-GENCY*, when Birdie flung herself at him and whunk! She smacked him over the head with her pocketbook. Sam went down. Only he hit the panel of buttons as he went, and galloping guppies! The elevator began tipping. It leaned over on its side and angled downward, which was about as much as we could tell shut up in such a solid box. It certain sure jumbled us all together in a heap. And man, we were moving downward fast. I couldn't even find the lighted numbers because everything was sort of mixed up. But I didn't need to see them to know something was happening.

Then the altitude, plus speed, plus the angle caught up with us. Frit-frat! We were weightless. One moment we were struggling to get out of the heap we'd landed in and the next moment we each shot off into different corners. A little effort really flings you around when you're weightless. Bong-bong, I bounced against the walls. Each time I tried to get straightened around, bong, I was off again. Mr. Cowboy still had his big hat on. It was jammed down around his ears and he had this funny expression on his face. "Unusual elevator," he said.

Boy, oh boy! Some people don't recognize an adventure when they're right in the middle of it. Birdie was kind of flying from one side to another, making little squeaky sounds. But suddenly a little common sense sifted through to my brain. If we were zooming downward, then pretty quick we'd hit the ground. At our speed we were going to get one, monstrous big jolt. I grabbed hold of Sam as he drifted by to try and shake him conscious and I shook myself into Sal who was swimming about with lazy, crazy swoops. Back I went to grab Sam. "Sam, Sam. Do something!"

And he did. He turned a beautiful lazy somersault. Obviously Sam was still out. It was up to me. I turned to the panel of buttons. Sam had hit something on the panel, but what? I pushed one of the buttons near the bottom. We zoomed downward still faster. I hung on and pushed one near the top. It felt as if we were changing direction. I twisted the *EMERGENCY* button and we flipped sideways. I felt myself drifting away from the panel, so I made this mad grab to stay put. Being weightless sure had problems all its own. Well, I got hold of something all right. The button for the door. Smooth as could be the doors each slid to the side and we found ourselves staring out the door. Only the door was in a wild place. It was where the floor should be. And there we were looking smack down on the Statue of Liberty and tugs and ships and ferries plowing along very properly.

Now can you explain to me why anybody would start weeping and moaning like a leaky faucet when something as gorgeous as New York's harbor was laid out below them? There's just no understanding adults. Birdie made a grab at her husband, and just about threw herself out the open door. It was lucky that Sal

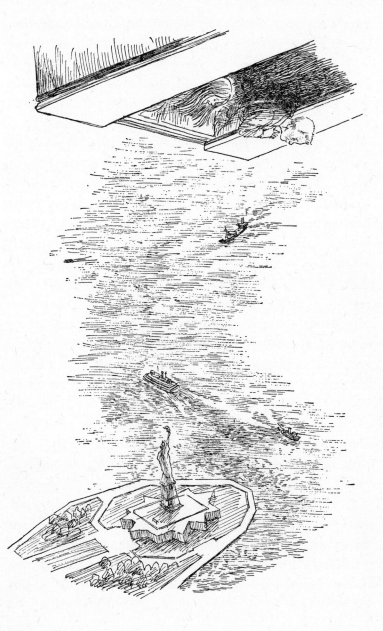

made a swoopy dive underneath her and pushed her upward.

Just about then, Sam seemed to snap to. "H'm-mmm," he said. And "Hummm," said he. And "Tut, tut, tut."

Right away he reached a hand up to the panel and pushed the hold button. We stopped right there, in mid-air. Next he pushed the button marked *Close door*. And the door closed. I hated to see that view end. But it had. Then he twisted the *EMERGENCY* button and the elevator began twisting until things were in their proper place. And next all of us bumped down to the floor like rocks. Our weightlessness had left.

"Now, Madam," said Sam to Birdie. He was very dignified in his manner. "I shall ask you to stop those disgusting, slobbering noises. I have a rule. When you have an adventure, make it first class. And above all enjoy it. Your sounds are ruining the pleasure for all of us."

Birdie made awfully strange sounds. I think she was trying to swallow her sobs. And she did. Mr. Cowboy reached down and put his arm around her. He kept shaking his head the way you do when something seems absolutely unbelievable. Maybe he wasn't used to her being so quiet. "Now, now, Birdie," he said. And then he spoke to Sam. "I surely don't understand why it should take us so long to reach the forty-fifth floor. A malfunction in the motor, I suppose."

Holy cow! He was really out of it. "I think we could agree on that," said Sam very pleasantly. "A malfunction. But I think we'd better take it in, Tryg. The magic is getting weak. We're on magic rations in my country. A shortage, you see."

"Shortages are occurring in everything," said Mr. Cowboy. And Birdie just stared.

Sam turned to the button panel again. Pushing first this, then that. I hated to see the fun ending. But let's face it. If the magic was going to run out, I'd just as soon not be in an elevator somewhere over Manhattan when it did. I felt the downward drift. And the numbers over the door began flashing again. Only now they were moving downward — 99 went by, 87, 77. When 65 came up, Sam pushed the *Hold* button. He turned toward the couple, and said, almost apologetically, "I don't want to frighten you, but I must be able to see outside for a moment so that I can come in on the shaft properly."

The doors slid open. It was something to see. The tops of the buildings were pointed toward the sky like giant fingers, all around us. Sam leaned out the door. Then turned back to the panel. And as the door was sliding shut, I saw them. A full formation of F 111's, the Swing Wing Navy planes, flashing toward us. I don't imagine they saw us because the sun was in their eyes. But frit-frat, can't you just see some pilots trying to explain about an elevator they sighted floating over downtown New York? I kind of smiled to myself as we started moving. Suddenly we jerked.

We jiggled. We jaggled. Almost like we were inside a giant concrete mixer. Overhead I could hear the jet engines as they zoomed past. Then the sounds vanished. The elevator stopped shaking. The floors began registering — 57, 56, 55. At 45 the elevator stopped. The door opened. And Mr. Cowboy led Birdie out. She was really hanging on to him. And he was saying the craziest thing. He said, "I know New York has remarkable things, but this elevator trip, it goes beyond what I expected."

And they were gone. "Sam," said Sal as the door closed, "let's do it again."

"No, child. Once is enough. It ruins the flavor of an adventure to repeat it."

It was the kind of thing adults usually say. I wasn't surprised. Still, it made a kind of sense. But obviously, Sal didn't agree. "We can too do it again." She yelled this at Sam.

Sam didn't bother to answer.

So Sal opened up with her blockbusting shrieks. Oh, I'd heard them before. It was a trick of Sal's to get her own way. Her shrieks always worked with Mom. And sometimes even with Dad. But they didn't faze Sam. He didn't even look at her. And right then the door opened at the main lobby. Standing outside the elevator was a mob of people. And in the front row were two elevator repair men. They looked grim. "Let them through. Let them through," they shouted.

They must have thought Sal was screaming from fright. Which was lucky. Sam started ahead. "Bring,

Sal, Tryg." He called it over his shoulder. "And do it now."

What a dilly of an order. Sal was not only screaming. She was lying flat on the floor kicking her feet. I moved toward her and heard one of the repair men say to Sam, "I wonder if you'd stop and talk to the manager, sir. There was a report that the elevator was missing from . . ."

He couldn't finish the sentence. I knew what he meant. Somebody must have taken a gander up the shaft and found the elevator gone. Only no normal, practical mechanic could put such a mad thought in words. Sam stopped short. He looked upset. I knew what Sam must be feeling — people persons are so rigid in their thinking. When he spoke, he almost sounded cross. "All right, all right." He had to shout to get above Sal's screams. "I'll go and see the manager. You children meet me in the lobby, Tryg."

I tried to shout after him that I needed help. But I didn't. Sam was like my Dad in some ways. When Dad told you to do something, he expected it done. I looked down at my screaming sister and had this deep urge to give her a solid kick. It's awfully hard sometimes not to give in to such an urge. But I held on. I noticed Sam stopping at a pillar and looking back. Boy! I knew what that meant. I'd better hop to it. I grabbed for Sal's hand. If I'd only looked at Sam at that moment I might have had a bit more confidence that I'd be able to handle Sal.

3

Sal Takes a Walk

Wʜᴇɴ ꜱᴏᴍᴇᴛʜɪɴɢ ʜᴀꜱ to be done, you might as well get it over with. Sal wasn't going to stop her screaming, because she was positive that Sam would give in. Well, she underestimated Sam. And I guess I underestimated him too. Because when I grabbed Sal's hand, a very peculiar thing happened. Her feet floated right up into the air. There she was like one of those gas balloons, trailing along after me. Sal was so surprised she stopped screeching. I was so surprised I let go. Whoompff! And there was Sal bumping along on the ceiling of the elevator. Which was pretty embarrassing. I could feel my face turning red to match my hair and more so. Outside in the lobby all these people were staring. Some were whispering. I heard a woman say, "How is he doing that?"

And somebody said. "They must be East Indians. I've heard they have powers of levitation."

Whatever that was, it didn't sound good. I didn't wait to hear more, but began reeling Sal in, like you pull a kite out of the sky, hand over hand. First I grabbed her foot, moved up to her knee, snagged her hand, and took off. People kept staring after us as if we were some kind of freaks. And that kid sister of mine. Darned if she didn't have this happy, tickled look on her face. Hey, Sam wasn't punishing her a bit. She was having a ball. I told her in a firm way to get her feet down on the floor. But she didn't. So I looked at the floor myself. That way I didn't have to look at anybody. But I could still hear. Things like, "Aren't they sweet." "I'm still asking how they're doing it?" "They must be foreigners." Things like that.

And then smack! I hit this solid obstacle — a man. A rather strange-smelling man. I mean he smelled as if he'd been drinking. At 12:30 in the afternoon? It didn't make much sense. And neither did Sal's antics because she was kicking her legs and bouncing about like a kite in the wind. This man grabbed hold of my T-shirt like he was drowning, got his face up close to mine and said, "Saaaay, fella . . ."

I hate having strangers grab at me. "Let go!" I said. I was trying to sound firm like a TV hero, but the words came out more like a shriek. My nerves were getting frazzled.

Well, my command worked all right, but not the way I had expected. The man hung on and Sal let go. And away she went — up, up, up, until her head was gently bobbing against the ceiling. I was lucky though, because the only people who saw her float off were the man and me. He almost fell over on his back, trying to keep track of her upward movement. Then frit-frat, that darn man let go of me which was great.

But he began to sob, great gulping sobs and call for a doctor. It sounded as if I'd done something to him.

I moved away from him quickly, trying to keep my eye on Sal who was moving in happy little dips and bobs along the ceiling of the Manor House lobby. Another obstacle moved in front of me. Yep, a man again. A very official-looking kind of man. Hefty, neatly dressed, oozing authority. "All right, Bud, what's going on here?"

It was a good question. I had a good answer too. "He made me lose my sister," I shouted. I have red hair and a temper to match. And at that moment my temper was at a sizzle. "That crazy man made me let go of my sister!"

"Now, now, lad, it can't be serious. I'm a detective. That's my business — finding people who get lost." Here I go again, another helpful uniform.

"It's not hard finding her," I said in a snotty way. "It's getting her that's hard."

"Let's go over that one again. You know where she is?"

"Of course I know where she is. Pardon me. I won't if I don't keep up."

I could see that Sal was floating out of the lobby with the reservation desk and into the one where the escalators went up and down to the second-floor ball-rooms. In the center of this room the ceiling went up two stories. Bob, bob, bob went Sal and disappeared. I ran. The detective ran. People turned to look at us.

"Sal, you come on down," I shouted. "You hear?"

"Can't come," her voice a little faint. "Heigh ho, heigh ho."

Galloping guppies! One day she doesn't talk and the next she's singing for an audience. Lucky that most people in the lobby never figured that the sound was coming from up above. So they didn't see Sal. Until this one woman riding down the escalator spotted her. "Merciful heavens!" she screamed.

And she pointed up, up, up at Sal who looked almost as if she were swinging on the draperies. The woman's pointing made the detective look up. And he said . . . I can't repeat what he said because I'm not supposed to repeat that kind of word, but he was startled. He was amazed. If detectives could faint, he probably was ripe for that action right then.

At which moment I saw Sam and rushed off toward him. "Hey, Sam." Then I muttered the next under my breath. "You're a little big, Sam. Seven feet is pretty big."

"Botheration," said Sam and began rubbing his wen.

"Not here. Not now," I said. "You want to scare these people to death?"

"Where's Sal?" asked Sam. ℔ SCHOOLS C711594

"Up in the air," I answered.

"Naturally," said Sam. "It's the usual female state. But I'd like a more definite answer to the question."

So I pointed. And almost stuck my finger in the detective's eye because he had chased right after me. He sounded as if he were trying to talk.

"Is that your little girl?" He finally squeezed out the words.

"Ah, so there she is," said Sam in a matter-of-fact tone as if little girls often floated up to the top of a ceiling.

"We're not debating where she is," yelled the detective. "We're trying to figure out how to get her down. And then I want to know how she got up there."

"Perhaps I ought to go after her," said Sam, sort of thinking out loud.

Talk about a wacky fairy godfather. Couldn't you see the excitement if he took off into the air too? "No, no, Sam! There's got to be another way." I got this comment in fast.

"A ladder!" shrieked a woman.

"Call the fire department!" yelled another.

I don't know where all the people were coming from, but we were suddenly in a mob. Hundreds and hundreds of people were pouring into the lobby and they were all staring up. From outside came the wail of a siren. Yikes! Somebody had really called the fire truck. But how could they get a fire truck inside? Weren't the long ladders attached to the trucks? A policeman was shouting at people to clear the way. For some time there had been this low roar of sound, a combination of all the voices of the people who were watching. They were saying things like, "But how did she get up there?" "Is that a balloon?" "No, no, it's a child." "Is she floating?"

Now with the arrival of official help a silence settled down, almost as if everyone were holding his breath. The firemen strode in. Sal looked down and waved excitedly and waved herself right off the drapery. A moan rose from hundreds of throats. Sal flipped herself over in a somersault and grabbed hold again. The crowd sighed all together like some huge monster. Considering that only yesterday Sal had been so shy that she wouldn't even speak to our milkman, her behavior ticked me off. Why, the rat, she was enjoying the excitement.

"I think," said Sam, "that there must be some logical way." He said this to me.

"I think you'd better think of it soon, before the whole city of New York gets in on the act," I said.

For the first few minutes the firemen stood there gaping, like the rest of the people were doing, because they are called on to rescue children in many odd situations, but I bet they'd never seen one playing on the ceiling two stories up. Someone yelled at Sal to be careful. Someone else shouted for her not to be afraid. Which was ridiculous. Sal was having too good a time to be afraid.

"Better do something, Sam — and quick," I said. Because I could kind of talk to him now without everyone listening. The firemen were crouched together, almost like a football huddle. They were trying to figure out their rescue action. If we were to get Sal down, it had to be now.

Sam evidently agreed, because he took off for the

escalator. I followed in his wake. It scared me to think of what he could do. If he sailed the escalator off to the ceiling — frit-frat! He'd really cause a sensation. But good old Sam! He actually acted in a very sensible way. When he got to the balcony he leaned over the railing, facing Sal. "Sal!" he called. Wow! When his voice boomed out, the windows sort of gave. No glass shattered, luckily. But that silence came down again. "All right, Sal, you hear me now?"

"Yes, Sam," said Sal in a very little voice.

"You are to walk on the ceiling, like a fly walks, upside down. Walk on the ceiling right over to me."

"I don't want to," said Sal.

Oh joy, here we went again. If Sal started screeching and yowling, I hated to think what would happen. I mean if Sam changed her into a toad or something how could I ever explain to my folks. Only right at this moment, she didn't even deserve to be a toad. But I needn't have worried. Sal did as she was told this time. She used the draperies to hang on to as she swung her feet higher and higher until they touched the ceiling. From down below us came these anxious sighs and squeals as very carefully Sal began walking toward us, her feet on the ceiling, her long hair dangling down toward the floor.

"You look funny," called Sal. "All upside down."

"You look a little upside down yourself," I shouted back.

Slowly she came toward us. "I'm getting dizzy,

Sam," she wailed. That was logical. When you're upside down for long the blood rushes into your brain. Why, she might black out. The thought scared me, because if she was unconscious and still stuck to the ceiling we'd have an awful problem. Luckily, she kept on coming. When she was almost to the balcony, Sam jumped up on the railing, reached up, grabbed Sal's hands and pulled her down, down. Then he cradled her in his arms. I couldn't hear whether he was scolding or praising her. But she had this sappy smile on her face. Then her head fell backward as if she'd passed out. Sam jumped down to the floor and moved to the escalator, with me right behind.

Down, down we went. As we stepped off Sam spoke to the mob pressing in upon him. "Clear the way, folks. Make way. The little girl needs air. Stand back, please."

And for heaven's sakes, people did step back. I don't know how they did it. But somehow a path was cleared. Sam walked us outside. And presto! He stepped into the first cab. "Central Park," he said and before anyone knew what was happening, the cab took off. It was almost as good as an escape in a spy movie. I couldn't resist looking back through the rear window as we pulled away. Crowds were pouring through the hotel doors, fighting each other to get through first. And leading the whole mob was the detective. I sure hoped I didn't run into him again. He could ask some pretty unanswerable questions. I turned myself round and looked at Sam who had the darnedest, smuggest smile on his face. You know, I think he had really enjoyed the excitement back at the hotel!

"Oh, Sam," I said.

He looked at me.

"You're still mighty tall, Sam."

"Botheration," said Sam. "What's all this fuss about size? Half the fun in life is having variety."

"People persons don't feel that way. Not about body size," I said. "They like to know what to expect in size when they meet a friend."

"Oh, all right then," said Sam, a little testily.

He began rubbing his wen and muttering something. And he began shrinking. Just a little bit. Sal was watching him, fascinated. But frit-frat, so was the cab driver. He was watching in his rear vision mirror. And next thing we knew the cab had hit the truck in front and an instant argument broke out between the drivers. The hassle was awful. Sam told me to pay our driver. We'd walk. That poor man was shook up all right. He said to forget it. And he had this worried look in his eye when he looked at Sam.

Sam grabbed Sal's hand and we started moving very quickly across the street. And there we were in Central Park. Which was lucky for us. Because we had had so much excitement that we couldn't have stood much of a hike. By the time we reached the duck pond, Sal was beginning to drag her feet. Next Sam picked her up in his arms and carried her. And then he said that maybe we'd better save the zoo for tomorrow. Which was a good idea, because Sal was sound asleep, her head on Sam's shoulder. And I was getting more tired by the minute.

Sam hiked us back to Fifth Avenue. We climbed on a bus and I paid. Always I paid. For a moment I was angry and then I realized that this was pretty silly. How many kids have flown over New York in an elevator or walked on a ceiling. I decided to count my blessings and quit the complaining. As long as I could, I'd pay. But what would happen when all the money was gone? There was a thought to chew on.

Only I didn't. I watched television for the rest of the afternoon. Sam whipped off to Ireland to check on our parents and came back with no news. He ordered hamburgers and french fries sent up for supper and we ate in our room. Next thing I knew it was bedtime. The end of our first day in New York. Well, it had really been a great day. I think I was still smiling when I went to sleep.

4

A First-Class Sandwich and Subway Ride

THE NEXT DAY started off as some days do — all
wrong! The first sound I heard was Sam talking on
the phone. He was ordering breakfast. Now I hate
to be a spoilsport, but I had arrived in New York
with about $25. Sam was spending my money as if
it were $500.

"Hey, Sam. Forget it, please. We can have a
doughnut."

And that's the way our grinchy morning began.
Sam told the operator to forget his order. Next he
turned and scowled at me. Then he sat down in the
big armchair and scowled at the ceiling. I felt a little
uneasy. After all, I didn't really know Sam very well.
Wonder if he got mad and left us now.

Even Sal had lost her bounce this morning. She
went about the business of getting dressed in a sober
way. She didn't hesitate and wonder what to wear.
She simply put on exactly what she had worn the day
before, so she looked a little messy. I took plenty of
time tying my shoes as if I could postpone a bit longer
telling Sam I was sorry, sorry to have butted in the
way I did when he was talking on the telephone. I

watched Sal struggling to brush her long hair. It was beginning to get a tangled, grapevine look, which didn't add to Sal's appearance.

And all this time Sam was not only scowling but grumbling. He was mumbling things to himself. All I could hear was the tone of his words, but not the words themselves. Still it didn't take any brain to figure out he was grumbling. I couldn't postpone the apology any longer. So I took a deep breath. "I'm sorry, Sam. I shouldn't have told you not to order breakfast."

Sam stopped mumbling. He looked at me. And galloping guppies! He smiled. "As I have told you, Tryg, when you have an adventure, make it first class. And don't be afraid to enjoy it. Still, it may be more adventuresome to eat a doughnut on the street. Come. We'll find out."

"I didn't mean to upset you," I said. His words hadn't penetrated my brain in the place where I understand. I was so intent on getting things right between us that I couldn't stop the apology.

Sam's look stopped me though. Because he was looking puzzled. "Upset? Ah yes, I am upset. But not at you, lad. At adults in your people person world. Adults are so, how would you say, unadaptable? They must always have things happen in the usual way."

I couldn't figure out what we were talking about. But I certainly agreed with Sam's comment. I was remembering how mad Mom had been when she

found I'd gone to school barefoot one day. And how
Dad had about had a fit when I put paprika on his ice
cream. Yep, adults liked things neat and ordinary,
that's for sure. Only what did this have to do with our
breakfast.

Sam went on. "I think you are both old enough to
understand." That remark really grabbed me in the
place where I get scared. Grown-ups always begin
this way when they're about to dish out bad news. "I
went to Ireland last night, just as I said I would. I
wanted to tell your parents where you were, that you
were safe, and having a fine time."

"You can say that again," I said quickly. Sal let out
a little squeal of agreement. "What did they say?" I
asked.

"I never got through. Communication takes open
lines, you see. Your parents resist anything they can't
understand. They do not understand magic or anything not explainable by known theories. I'm afraid
they wouldn't hold with fairy godfathers. They met
each attempt of mine to reach their minds with anger
and worry and static. I do not think they understood.
Mainly they seemed to be only concerned, frantic
perhaps describes their attitude, to get on a plane.
From the way they were demanding space, I would
expect them to arrive today. Meanwhile, should we
go adventuring? We have only a little time left, I
fear."

"Oh, yes, Sam, let's go." That was Sal. Her bounce
was coming back. I think that down underneath she

was a little homesick for Mom, but now that she was coming Sal could enjoy herself.

"I'm ready," I said. But I didn't sound as happy as Sal did. It was a queer thing. I should have been tickled by Sam's announcement that our folks might arrive today. But I wasn't. I felt a real deep twinge of regret. And a need to hurry, hurry into the day's activities, because our time was running out.

This turned out to be Sam's day for walking us. Man! I've never hiked like that before and we've taken some long hikes in our scout troop. Maybe the New York pavement made the distance seem longer. The heat radiated from the concrete and you could almost feel your feet cooking. So what did we see? About everything there was in Central Park, I think. If my feet are any gauge. Sam took us through the greenhouses and the zoo. He let Sal and me walk through the kiddy zoo where the animals live in funny little houses and the fountain is a whale shooting water from his spout. Soon my feet were not only hot, they were beginning to hurt in so many places that all I could think was ouch! ouch! ouch! I suggested we try a ride in a horse-drawn carriage. But wouldn't you know, Sam decided to be economical. He said it cost too much money. Galloping guppies! He acted at times just like a people person grown-up. Sam was willing to spend money as long as it was his idea.

I felt grumpy all the way through and bit by bit I dropped behind Sal and Sam. I began to think that Sam was going to hike us around until we were well cooked by the July sun. I heard Sal asking for a box of popcorn. Guess who paid for that? Me, of course. And then that dumb kid goes and feeds the stuff to the ducks. She and Sam were absolutely revolting standing at the edge of the pond and giggling at the ducks as they went through mad antics to get the popcorn. If I hadn't been so grumpy, I might even have enjoyed the ducks diving and scrambling and squawking myself.

Instead I took off my shoes and stockings and dipped my feet into the water. What bliss! Until the policeman sailed up and gave me what-for because wading wasn't allowed in that pond. Who was wading? Not me, that's for certain sure. But I knew better than to get us into trouble with the law by arguing. I put on my shoes feeling grinchier than ever. And then Sam came up with a great idea. He said, "Let's eat."

Up to that minute I hadn't even realized that I was hungry. But as soon as Sam suggested food, my mouth began to react. And it felt great to know that the only thing wrong with me was an empty stomach. After all a doughnut doesn't stick with you too long. Well, Sam surprised us again. He started walking us. That was no surprise. But he walked us to Park Avenue and then up a side street. And frit-frat, he led us down some stairs into the basement of a building and through the door of something called a sandwich shop. This was a sandwich shop with a difference. The whole thing was about the size of my grandma's cedar closet and it had a serving table like a cafeteria. I bet it was about the smallest cafeteria in the world. Only the choices you got to make were for sandwich fillings. You could have a sandwich made to order. What a dreamy idea. Sal went absolutely mad. She began with a submarine-shaped bun, a huge thing. Then on it she had a layer of tuna fish salad, a slice of ham, a slice of American cheese, some pickle relish, a little hot chili, and a big glob of ham salad on top. The fellow behind the counter never blinked an eye. I guess in New York, nobody is surprised at anything. Of course, I understood why later when he totaled up the bill. Why should he worry if some kid was nuts. It all led to profit for him.

I shouldn't criticize Sal, though, because my sandwich was almost as wild. It had a slab of roast beef, sauerkraut, Swiss cheese, a smidgin of Sloppy Joe filling, lettuce, a huge dill pickle, and a layer of peanut butter. Sam took nothing. He had explained before how our food was simply not the kind of food he ate. So the clerk dropped our sandwiches into a brown paper sack, added two cartons of milk that Sam insisted we have, and handed me the register receipt. I focused my eyes on the numbers, but nothing registered in my brain. Nothing sensible, that is. I thought the numbers added up to $5.35 which was ridiculous. Then I knew it wasn't ridiculous. It was for real. I thought of asking the man if we could take off a few things, but when my brain began to function again, I knew that nobody was about to take back some chili-flavored American cheese or soggy roast beef. Slowly I counted out the money. And I tried desperately not to notice how little was left. As Sam had said, if you're going to have an adventure, enjoy yourself.

So I enjoyed myself. Sitting on a park bench I savored each separate layer of the sandwich which somehow blended together into a wonderful taste. Once I was full I was too comfortable to worry. I did mention to Sam, very casually as we walked toward a bus line, that we'd better go easy on the money. But he didn't seem to listen. He said the same, dumb old thing — something would turn up. I hoped it would turn up soon.

At the bus stop, Sam helped us in. He said something to the driver, but it wasn't until we stepped off that I realized Sam was taking us to the Guggenheim Museum. I started to protest. How much can one pair of feet take. But protesting to Sam always turned out about as satisfactory as arguing with the wind. Sam said he felt we needed some culture as well as fun. So that was that.

Only it didn't seem quite fair to me. I was the only one who got the culture. After the first few steps up that circular ramp, Sal conked out. And Sam carried her. She slept the whole blessed way. But I got a non-stop, intensive lecture on Calder as we climbed up and up to the top. I didn't admit it to Sam, but this guy Calder really came up with some fascinating mobiles. Made me think about going home and trying a few myself.

It was late when we got out on the sidewalk. Almost five o'clock and about half the people in New York seemed to be out in front of the museum, hurrying, hurrying somewhere. Ever get caught in a stampede of people rushing to get home? I bet a buffalo stampede has nothing on this one. Didn't bother Sam a bit. But then he had an advantage. When he saw the mob, he rubbed that bump on his nose, said some words under his breath and grew a bit. When you get a mass of man some six feet, six inches tall, in a wild-looking costume, you've got a sure-fire, mob-breaker-upper. Sam moved along like a bulldozer going through butter. People melted before him. I

couldn't figure out where we were going until we reached a stairway going down. Galloping guppies! A subway. Sam must be taking my worry about the money to heart. Only with the late afternoon heat and the crush of people, I rather wished he hadn't.

Sam got us down the steps, through the turnstiles, and onto the platform. A train roared in. And then an interesting thing happened, almost like a game. Everybody on the platform rushed for the doors when they opened. And the people inside rushed to get out. The two masses met. There was a moment when nothing seemed to be happening. The glob of people quivered and shook. Then as if by signal, almost like magic, the pressure released. And the crowd flowed in both directions, and we were inside.

Right about then somebody gave Sam a blow to his

midriff. I suppose that's what happened, because Sam let out a kind of outraged gasp. He lowered Sal to the floor. Lucky girl! She now had a terrific view of people's rumps and pocketbooks and assorted packages. "Sam."

It was a very little sound, but you could tell Sal was in trouble. She could hardly breathe. She had been clutching her Daffy bear in her hand and somehow it had gotten wedged between a fat woman's stomach and a man's trousers. When poor Sal tried to pull Daffy loose, both people scowled at her.

I was beginning to feel a bit like pressed sausage myself. I could see Sam struggling to get his hand up from his side where it was trapped. Frit-frat! He was rubbing his wen and I could tell his lips were moving even though I couldn't hear any sounds. Next thing I noticed was that I could breathe better. A space seemed to be clearing around us. People were muttering at other people about not shoving. One man was threatening to give another a good punch in the nose. And there was a general angry hum, but people kept moving back. Because something was pushing them back, back until there was a nice clear space around Sal and Sam and me. Almost a foot in each direction. Naturally some people tried to move in. Oh, they tried all right, but they didn't make it. Instead they shoved against the people on the outside edge who got fighting mad. Looked as if we might get a first-class fight or two. The conductor stuck his head in the door at each stop and shouted, "Move up in front! Move up in front there."

He seemed to be mainly talking to us. So Sam was agreeable. He moved. Oh, Sam could be accommodating all right. But our nice clear space moved right with us. Which crowded the people on all sides until still more people were muttering and shouting and demanding that everyone stop the pushing. Everywhere, everywhere it was hot! Hot! HOT! The fans turned but about all they were doing was to whip the hot air in your face. It was a long ride wherever we were going. Sam never bothered to say. When South Ferry Station was called Sam started toward the door. And you know something. Our neat little space moved with us. One man got pushed into a woman's lap and she smacked his face. Some kids had to climb up on the back of the seat to avoid being squashed. That air really had pressure.

Then we were on the platform and with Sam leading the way we moved out and toward another building. It looked like some kind of depot or station. Certainly wasn't very exciting, that's for sure. Which shows how wrong you can be. I should have known that whatever Sam had in mind was bound to be an adventure.

5

A Fairy and a Ferry

You KNOW WHAT that building was that Sam was herding us into? A ferry station. No, it had nothing to do with fairies. Not Sam's kind of fairies. These were boats that go back and forth between Manhattan and Staten Island. Hey, how's that for excitement? A boat ride. Sal began to burble, she was so excited, and her eyes turned deep purple as they do when she's especially happy. Sam showed us how to go through the turnstiles. Lucky for me that the fare was only five cents apiece. After that lunch I had panicky feelings about spending any money. And there we were on the boat. It had outside places to sit, benches, of course. And then there was a protected spot to sit inside and they even had a hot dog stand there.

First we rode across, watching boats whiz by us, the little boats, you know. Tugs went by hauling a mammoth ocean liner up the sound. And of course, the Statue of Liberty was standing on her little island, torch held high. The lady surely looked different from this level than she had when we were floating over her in the elevator. Once we had tied up at the other dock, everybody flowed off. We waited until the crush was over, then walked off, and lined up to get back on. There went another fifteen cents. But for the kind of ride we were getting, it would be awfully silly tc complain.

About this time the smell of those hot dogs really got to me. I asked Sam if we could each have one and he thought it most sensible. So we tried a hot dog, New York style, I'd call it. The woman put on ketchup and mustard and pickle and galloping guppies! She added sauerkraut. I was a little squeamish about try-ing it. But not Sal. She bit right in as if she always had her hot dogs trimmed up this way. I waited a minute for her reaction. Well, she didn't drop dead, so I tried it myself. I had nothing to lose but my lunch. I bit.

Talk about super wonderful. What a flavor. What a taste. Once I had started I couldn't seem to chew fast enough. It was that good. Sal and I couldn't resist. We had to have another. And another. Which suited Sam just fine. He said the combination gave us meat, starch, and vegetable so to eat all we wanted. That was a surprise, to find something that we liked and that a grown-up approved. Sal stopped with three of the things and I had four. I might have eaten five, but a little warning bell sounded somewhere in my brain. I had the feeling that maybe I had better count my money.

Which I did. Holy cow! I only had about $1.50

left. And that scared me a bit. Sam could talk about
something turning up, but it looked to me as if the
only thing that was going to turn up was the police
when we couldn't pay our bills. "Sam." I pulled at his
coat to get his attention. He was leaning on the railing looking out at the Manhattan skyline. I stopped to
look too. Because it was something to see. The sky
had this luminous orange glow and the tall buildings on
Wall Street looked like some dream city that had
sprung up.

Then I got down to business. I jerked Sam's coat
again. He looked at me, a little surprised. Now that
I had his attention what could I say. I didn't want
him to think I didn't trust him about finding us some
money. But I couldn't escape the feeling that fairy
godfathers weren't very practical in the people person
world. There was no easy way to say it so I blurted out
the words. "Sam, we're broke."

"Tut, tut, tut," said Sam. He rubbed a little bit at
his wen, looking very thoughtful. I held my breath
hoping that maybe silver dollars or dimes would
come pouring out of his pocket, his mouth, his ears.
But nothing dramatic like that happened. In fact,
nothing happened.

"We've got to get off," I said sadly. "We can't keep
riding because riding is costing us money."

"I don't want to get off. Please, Sam, I don't want
to get off," said Sal, but she didn't holler it. She was
very polite. Except her eyes began to fill with tears
and I heard a little sniff. Darned if Sal wasn't about

to cry. Well, that was good. Crying I can handle, but bellowing scares the living daylights out of me.

"We have to get off," I said, firmly I hoped.

"But wonder," said Sam, "wonder if we could ride without it costing us money?"

I thought that would be a real wonder, but I didn't say so. Because right then I noticed Sam was rubbing his wen and muttering. "Oh, Sam," said Sal. The way she was looking at him you felt a fire must be burning in her insides. "Sam are you going to make us invisible?"

"Botheration," said Sam. "Why didn't I think of that? Well, it's too late now. We're stuck with my idea. Though it's a whing-dinger of an idea if I do say so myself."

At which moment the engines slowed down, you could hear their sound changing to a low rumble. We were about to dock on the Manhattan side. But, holy cow! Nothing happened. The engines were chugging. The water was spraying by. And there the ferry sat. About twenty feet from the dock. It never got farther away but it never came closer either. Then the ferry did some fancy zigging and then a little zagging as if by coming in at a different angle we could make it to the dock. But no! The dock was where the dock always had been and the ferry was where it seldom had been, twenty feet out. Oh, boy! Talk about excitement. Passengers were beginning to get a little nervous and I had this overwhelming desire to laugh out loud at all of them, because they were silly enough to expect the usual when Sam Bottleby was aboard.

Next the captain tried some fancy little darts. I think that's what he was attempting. And he was about as successful as someone teaching an elephant to do ballet. The people on the deck had stopped being surprised. They were angry. And they were hollering, shouting, screeching at the crew to do something. As if they weren't trying. Ah, that Sam, he really had had a whing-dinger of an idea this time.

A few moments later the Coast Guard ship came zooming in toward us. What a beautiful, sleek boat. The light on top was whirling and flashing and the siren was going full blast. They slid in beside us neat as could be and some sailors threw a tug rope to the ferry's crew. Obviously they were going to pull us into the dock. Looked like the fun was over. But that shows how wrong I was. Because no matter how much oomph the Coast Guard ship applied, the ferry stayed that same twenty feet out. Whenever it reached that twenty foot point it balked and jumped and bounded like an untamed bronco. It tossed all of us about a little. By now some of the passengers were hollering and wailing as if they were about to be killed. Yep, it's a sad fact that most grown-ups don't recognize an adventure when they're having it. Most of the passengers seemed interested only in getting off. So finally the Coast Guard did just that, took them off in small boats. But not us. Why, we wouldn't have missed the fun for anything. I wondered what the crew would do next.

We didn't have to wait long, because we backed off from the Manhattan dock and started toward the Staten Island side, with the Coast Guard ship slicing along beside us. I don't know what plan was underway. Listening to the men talk you could tell the whole thing was very confusing. Someone even suggested that there was a magnetic field holding the boat from landing. That was an interesting idea, especially as none of the other ferries were having a bit of trouble landing.

Naturally, at the other side, the situation was exactly the same. The ferry couldn't land. Someone had called in tugs and now they attached lines to the ferry. Those tugs chugged, pulled, struggled. And the harder they chugged, pulled, struggled, the harder Sam rubbed at his wen. All of which made the ferry buck, bounce, and moan. But it still stayed twenty feet out. One of the ferries got grounded and we had the fun of watching them pull it loose. But otherwise the situation remained the same.

Then somebody had the bright idea that fireboats might be able to drive us in with water. Hey! Talk about fun. The fireboats came roaring in with sirens going full blast. And a regular water battle began. Huge jets of water from their hoses were directed at the rear of the ferry, just above the water line. There was water, water everywhere. Onlookers at the ferry

dock were shouting and yelling like they were cheer-
leaders for the Green Bay Packers, urging them to
hit the line. We sure hit something. For a minute I
thought we might be airborne. There was water going by in every direction. Sam was grumbling about
hating to get wet and rubbing his wen like mad. Then
it was over. Oh, it wasn't that the ferry had moved
but simply that the fireboats gave up.

By now we were getting lots of attention from other
boats in the area. They began clustering around, everybody shouting at the nearest ear trying to find
out what was happening. Nobody, but nobody, could
believe the story that the ferry couldn't get into the
dock. It was wonderful. Sam's idea was a whing-
dinger all right. But then Sam was that kind of person. He had the greatest ideas.

In sheer desperation, the captain decided to try the
Manhattan side again. By now the photographers
and reporters had arrived in small craft which kept
dodging in and out. Nobody would permit them on
the ferry. We were pretty exclusive riding up there
by ourselves. It was almost dark by now. The sun
was gone and only an afterglow showed in the sky
making the tall buildings stand out like drawings made
by some kid. The ride back across the sound was exciting, because we had a regular parade of big and
little boats, all with their lights showing fore and aft
and all with people shouting helpful advice to whoever might be listening. Advice like, "Get a helicop-
ter." "Blow it up." "Use a laser ray." The advice was

marvelously unhelpful. And Sam sat there on one of the benches, watching the rosy sky, and rubbing his bump in a very thoughtful way. I could hear the motors revving up as we neared the dock. The power must have been turned on full. If Sam's magic weakened now — help! We might be driven right through the dock. But good old Sam held the boat the same twenty feet out. Only the impact when we hit the solid wall of nothing threw Sal and me smack off our feet. We lay there for a moment, dazed. And then I noticed Sam was walking away from us. Only it wasn't the Sam I had become used to seeing, you know, crazy deep-topped boots, tight trousers, plaid jacket. Nope, Sam had on some uniform.

My curiosity has always been super-sized. I had to find out what he was up to. So I followed along. I found out quickly enough. First off, the Coast Guard seamen who had boarded the ferry to give its crew a hand saluted Sam smartly. And the next thing, I heard the captain call Sam "Admiral." That was like Sam. He believed in making an adventure first class. So naturally he'd be an Admiral. I wondered, though, if he knew the penalty for impersonating a United States officer. And the thought scared me. But Sam wasn't worried. Not Sam. He spoke in a very gruff, Admiral-like voice. "All right, men. What's going on here?"

Well, everybody tried to tell him at once. The captain was saying that the engines were set "Full speed ahead" and we were standing still. A Coast Guard officer was describing how ten towing ropes had been snapped. Somebody else was explaining about the water bath idea. Sam listened to everything, very thoughtfully. Then he stared at them, his eyes snapping. Boy! I knew that look. You didn't argue with Sam when he looked at you that way. And the men reacted just as I had expected. Fact is, I've never seen a group of men look more scared and shook up. Still how often do ordinary New York seamen see an Admiral? Especially an Admiral like Sam.

Just as Sam was about to spit out an order, Sal came stumbling into the wheelhouse room. She grabbed Sam's hand and held on in this dazed way. I think the jolt when we hit that pressure wall going full tilt had jumbled up her thinking.

"Can we go see the ocean, Sam," she begged. "See the ocean and then go home."

I gulped. The men stared. Somebody began to protest. But Sam? Sam registered nothing. He acted as if this were the most sensible thing he had heard. "Good idea, men. The child has a fine idea. I should have thought of it myself. The ship is obviously being held down by some variety of salitashus, obligatus isotopes. We will move out to the ocean. Clean off these elements in ocean water. And then sail back to land. And that's an order, men." Wow! Sam barked out those last words.

Well, nobody argues with an Admiral, nuts or not. The men did what they were told. The ferry backed out from the dock. The people on the shore were shouting questions. Automobile horns were blasting like mad as we started toward the sea. There were probably some very surprised people in the small boats bounding around us. But they weren't daunted by the change of pattern. Nope, they fell in behind us so that we looked like some Pied Piper for small boats. And what a mish-mash of sound. Some people on the other boats were playing guitars and singing. Others had tapes that blatted out electric sounds of drums and trumpets and guitars. It was great. Absolutely

great, like some huge winding ribbon of happy noise.

Twilight was fast disappearing into darkness. The Coast Guard ship with revolving lights turning and spotlights playing over our decks kept pace beside us. I think they were afraid we might disappear. Sal fell asleep. It had been a long day. And Sam promptly ordered the ferry to turn about. Which it did. We sailed back to the dock and landed very neat and properly as a ferry should. I bet everybody else was surprised. But not me. I knew it would happen.

You should have seen those officers and men salute as Sam, decked out in his Admiral's uniform, strode past them to the dock. He was carrying Sal who wouldn't wake up no matter how much he jiggled her. Photographers' flashbulbs were popping and reporters were crowding around shouting questions. Sam kind of glared them into silence. "You are disturbing my godchild, young man," he said to one man. "Stand back, sir," he said to another.

Oh, Sam could be awesome. He was in such a hurry he almost shoved me smack through the cab instead of into it. And when he ordered the driver to get going, that driver got going in a hurry.

But not for long. Because, galloping guppies! Sam had suddenly remembered the need for economy. He told the driver to drop us at the nearest subway station. Which he did. I guess economy is a great thing to practice but it does seem awfully hard on the feet at times. Man, oh man! That hike from the subway station in Times Square to our hotel stretched out almost forever. I was barely moving when we reached the entrance to the Manor House. Sam stopped abruptly. He put Sal down, gave her a little shake, turned to me and handed over the key. "I'm late, Tryg. It's time for me to report in. You take the key. And both of you get right to bed. See you in the morning."

Before I could even say "Sam," he was gone. Sal and I started toward the elevators, moving like a pair of zombies. We were standing there waiting for one to come down when I felt funny bumps at the back of my neck like somebody was staring or talking about me. I turned around. Frit-frat! There was a group gathered at the desk. And they were looking our way. But worst of all, one of them was that detective who had found Sal walking on his ceiling. We had to move. I could imagine the kind of questions he might ask and I wasn't in very good shape for answering.

I didn't just step into the elevator. I bounded in, dragging Sal along, shoved the button, and away we zapped. But I didn't push the button for our floor. Nope, I pushed floor 45 which meant we had five flights to walk. But luckily it was all downhill or we'd never have made it. I quickly opened the door and we fell into bed. And my last little thought before falling asleep was, "Man! It has been a wonderful day."

6

A Hair-Raising Fling

"Take your foot off me!!!"

Those were the first words I heard the next morning. Yikes! Did I ever jump. Because the words were coming right out of the carpet. I was hopping out of bed when all the ruckus began. You know who it was, of course. It was Sam. Good old Sam Bottleby. But a smaller Sam Bottleby than I'd ever seen. You've heard the description "knee-high to a grasshopper." I'm not sure Sam would have even reached a grasshopper's knees.

"Galloping guppies, Sam! Whatcha doing? I could have smashed you." My temper flared suddenly, because if I had hurt Sam, even accidentally, I'd have felt awful.

There was this flash of wind, almost as if someone had rushed by me. Which is not surprising. Because someone had rushed by me. Sam, naturally. Only he was not going by in a usual way, he was going by me up and down. He grew so fast, he created a draft. It startled me so that I fell over backward into bed. Sal thought the whole thing terribly funny. She sat there shaking and hooting. Girls, honestly!

And Sam, about six feet four, stood there towering over me, his beard so bright, his hair so flaming that I was really seeing red. Suddenly the whole thing seemed so ridiculous that I started to laugh. And that's the way the day began.

Sam reported that he had checked on our parents. And they were still in Ireland, still trying to get on a plane. "So we have the day to ourselves. What shall we do?" he asked. "Baseball? Tour of the U.N.? A play?"

Sal bent her head over her knees. She thought best that way, and for the first time I looked at her, really looked at her. She was an absolute mess. Her long hair was tangled like a bramble thicket. You couldn't tell where it began or ended. It didn't seem to bother Sal. "I'd like, I'd like, I'd like to see my Mommy and Daddy," said Sal.

There was logic for you. Course, knowing Sam, Sal probably figured anything was possible. "H'mmm," said Sam. He thought for a few moments and when he began rubbing at his nose, I got a whole bunch of delicious tingles running up my spine. Only Sam stopped the rubbing, and shook his head. "No! No! I don't want to use up our ration of magic on a trip. Can't see that it would help a thing."

"You mean," I said slowly because I couldn't get used to the idea, "you mean that you get only a certain amount of magic each day?"

"So to speak, so to speak. Have to use judgment

about when and when not to use it. Can't see how dropping in briefly on your parents could possibly benefit anyone, adults being what they are. I'm afraid the whole thing would alarm them." I had to agree with him on that point. "No, I think it best to let things ride as they are." He stopped again and looked at us thoughtfully. Which made us look at each other. And frit-frat! I could see why Sam was staring. We hadn't even bothered to take off our shoes last night when we jumped into bed. No wonder Sam had worried that I was going to smash him when I bounded out this morning. Bare feet can hurt plenty but with my heavy shoes on I could have clobbered him.

"First things first," said Sam. He kind of smiled at us. Why, he thought it was funny. Sam was awfully unpredictable. So are most grown-ups. "First thing in this case is for both of you to get out of yesterday's clothes, wash, and put on fresh things. Meantime, I'll order breakfast. And then I believe I'll just fly over to Ireland and try to communicate with your parents again. They might be more receptive. I'll assure them that all is well. Don't have much faith in its working, but I'll try."

And then Sam said, "Tut, tut, tut." I knew something was up. I stopped untying my shoelaces and looked up at Sam who was looking very intently at Sal. Oh, oh, he had seen Sal's hair. I was sure glad Mom couldn't see it at this minute because she always kept it so smooth and silky, she'd be about sick. Sal looked like she was studying to be a madwoman or a witch. Then I glanced back at Sam and galloping guppies! Sam was looking at me. You know the kind of look. I got the message right quick.

"Oh, no, you don't," I said. "You're not going to get me to comb out that little monster's hair. We'd be in a smackeroo of a fight first thing. The minute Sal felt a twinge of hurt she'd haul off and sock me. Which would mean I'd have to sock her and there we'd be." I felt this was a fair picture of what would happen, knowing Sal and me. "Besides," I added, "I bet I could work all day and never get that bramble bush combed out."

"Hmm," said Sam. And "H'mmmm," again. "I think you have made a fair evaluation of the situation so we won't attempt to comb it out."

Oh, oh . . . whenever a grown-up agrees with you, look out. That's one of the first rules you learn as a kid. I swallowed. I had a feeling I wasn't going to like what was coming. And I didn't. "I think," said Sam, "that the best solution is to cut Sal's hair short."

"Hey!" That word exploded from me. "Wait a cotton-picking minute. Mom would have a fit. She loves Sal's hair long. And Sal's proud of it herself. She'd never let me cut off even a smidgin. Would you, Sal?"

"Yes, I would," said Sal, nodding her mop of hair agreeably.

That's like my kid sister. Instant agreement with the exact opposite of what I had said. So there went my support. But I wouldn't give up. "I can't cut her hair, Sam, because I don't know how. And besides that, I don't even have any scissors." I folded my arms across my chest feeling very triumphant at finding such solid reasons for not cutting Sal's hair.

"Scissors," said Sam. "Why didn't you mention scissors before? I just happen to have a pair right here in my vest pocket."

And with a flourish he pulled out these weird blades and handles. They were in two parts, you see, which didn't look too useful to me. On each blade, one side was bumpity like a razor blade and the other side looked swoopy, curved-like. The handle was a little odd too because the grip wasn't solid as grips usually are. Instead it looked as if it were made of leather, leather gathered up with a drawstring.

"Those are scissors?" I asked.

"Of course, they are scissors," said Sam a little crossly. "Now if I could just find the nut."

Ohhhh, how I wanted to say, "Why, here's the nut," and point right at him. But I had this feeling that Sam could get uppity about such a bratty remark. I said nothing. Every now and then I show I've got a few brains.

Sam did find the nut. He got the scissor thing screwed together and they looked a little more like the usual kind. Then he handed them to me. Ever been grabbed by a pair of scissors? That's the only way I can describe it. Those gathered-up holes that served as the handle actually squeezed my thumb and forefinger when I took hold. I thought I was going to lose the circulation in my hand, that's the kind of squeeze I was feeling. The whole thing scared me. I jerked them off my fingers and heaved them across the room.

"Tut, tut, tut, Tryg. I never again want to see such a display of fright at the unusual. These are superb scissors. They cannot hurt you. Now go and get cleaned up. Eat your breakfast when it comes. And then I want you to cut Sal's hair. And that is an order, Tryg. I'll be back in a trice."

I was so busy trying to figure out what a trice was that I didn't notice that Sam had gone. But both Sal and I hopped to it and did as ordered. When our breakfast came we had no difficulty at all following Sam's directive to eat. It was another glorious, wonderful meal. I took my time eating. Partly because I was trying to postpone that hair-cutting chore. But it was awfully hard to postpone it any longer when the waiter removed the table and empty dishes. There was no excuse left. So on with the miserable job. First I tied a towel around Sal's neck. She was awfully helpful. Too helpful. Because the next thing she did was to crawl over the bed and dig up the scissors from the spot that they'd landed in, the wastebasket. Good riddance was my feeling. And do you know what she said when she picked them up by the handles? "They cuddle, the scissors cuddle."

Help! What a nauseating description. Accurate but nauseating. I grabbed them out of her hand fiercely and began chopping away at the mess of hair. Snip, snap, snurr the scissors sang. Around her head I marched, trying to cut off a few inches first. I never looked behind me. I had to concentrate on where I was going. When I got back to where I had started, my eyes felt as if they were popping out of their sockets. Holy cow! Sal's hair was longer than when I had begun. But that was impossible. I looked at those scissors, thinking, and then back at the hair. I'd cut off a couple of feet this time. I'd show that hair. And I rushed at the job. I think Sal thought I was going to pull it out by the roots I was using so much steam. Snippity, snappity, snoppity. I made it completely around again.

Oh, no! The hair was hanging below the chair. Frit-frat! That hair was growing faster than I was cutting it off. Well, no hair of Sal's was going to get ahead of me. I went at it again with gusto. Sal began to whimper. My mad energy was beginning to scare her. Then she started in giggling which didn't make sense. I like people to be consistent in their reactions. Either laugh or cry but don't do both at once.

"You're tickling," she managed to gasp out.

"The heck I'm tickling. You're doing it to yourself. It's your hair." Which was the truth.

I was beginning to feel a little desperate because the hair was gaining on me. It was snicker-snackering right down Sal's legs. About the longest hair I'd ever seen. But Sal wouldn't let me cut any more right then. She insisted on seeing herself in the mirror. So we started across the room. First she fell into

a three-foot pile of hair and giggled up a storm. Sal's
awfully ticklish. I got her moving again and when
she saw herself she couldn't believe it. Sal's hair
was long enough by now to wear it as a train. It might
be an interesting way to wear it I thought, trailing
along behind.

But I didn't think that thought long. "Do something." Sal was panicked. She kept screaming, "Do
something. I'll smother."

How ridiculous can you get? There wasn't a chance. But I began cutting like crazy. And I kept on cutting until I had her hair in huge piles tumbling over the coffee table, packed against the beds, under the beds, even on top of the beds. I was wondering if we'd have to move out into the hall for storage space. It might take some explaining to the maid. Then I heard that familiar, "Tut, tut, tut! What's going on here?"

And there at last was Sam. "Help!" I said it very weakly. I was beginning to feel exhausted. "Sal's hair won't stop growing."

"So I see. So I see. H'mmm." Sam took the scissors from my hand and they put up no fight. I was glad they let go. Well, he stood there looking at them and thinking. "Ah," he said, "of course. I have the blades reversed. Which stimulated rather than stopped the hair's growth."

Wouldn't you know that Sam would have crazy scissors like that? I had hardly finished thinking this thought when Sam had finished unscrewing the blades and putting them together backward. "I'll finish the job," he said. "I often cut the pixies' hair at home. It's a hobby of mine. So I'll give you a pixie cut, Sal."

He got no argument from me. I was glad to be through with the job. Well, Sam cut away swiftly at Sal's hair. And it fell neatly to the floor, exactly as one usually expects hair to fall to the floor. Once cut, the hair on Sal's head stayed that way. Sam certainly knew what he was doing. When he had finished, I could hardly recognized my sister, Solveig. She was that different. I almost thought her nose turned up now that her hair was so short and perky.

"It's great, Sam. Hey, that haircut is really great!" I said. And I meant it.

Sal went bouncing about clapping her hands and oohing and ahing. At herself, of course. I think you could describe her reaction as ecstatic, though I haven't seen too many ecstatic reactions, so I'm not sure. Snap went Sam's fingers. I could tell. An idea had been born. "Of course," he said, "that's it."

He was looking at those piles of Sal's hair which certainly did not inspire me with any thoughts except dull ones such as how we'd have to clean up the mess and get rid of it. "Don't you see, Tryg, Sal? Our money is right here," said Sam.

"Right where?" asked Sal.

That was a good question. "The hair, in the hair," said Sam.

Sal threw herself at the piles of hair and began giggling madly. I guess she thought there were silver dollars or at least fifty-cent pieces buried in the stuff. And all she found were giggles. Sam explained what he meant. He said we could sell Sal's hair. There were a lot of wigmakers in New York who'd pay well for human hair. Sam sure knew a lot about our human activities. But I didn't care a bit.

Let's not go into those next hours. They were filled with work and lots of it. We packed Sal's hair into pillow cases. I think Sam had probably lifted them from the linen cupboard when the maid wasn't looking. Sam could be very thoughtful. You can imagine what a fright the maid would have had if she'd seen a whole stack of pillow cases floating out the door and up the hall. Next we had to get the dozen cases stuffed with hair down to the first floor. Sam insisted we take the freight elevator. He said it was more proper. Then we had to find a cab and this worried me, because I wondered where we'd get the money. But Sam came through. He had a little left over from last night's ride. Luckily the first wigmaking place was close at hand.

Boy, the scene at that wig factory was really something. I don't suppose that it's an everyday event to have a red-bearded giant and two children come in lugging a dozen pillow cases filled with long, and I do mean long, brown hair. All of it amazingly alike. The manager couldn't believe that it was human hair. He tested it. He questioned us. But we were all very vague. Even Sal. We knew if we got trapped that the truth would be awkward. Unbelievable is probably a better description. But that Sam! He couldn't let things go along calmly. He told the manager that we'd been experimenting with raising hair.

"Raising hair?" asked the man.

"Yes, raising it. Stimulating growth, so to speak," said Sam.

I had kind of a hunch that he was enjoying the baffling conversation.

"This hair has not been permanented or dyed?"
asked the buyer.

"Oh no," piped up Sal. "My mommy would never
let me do that."

"Your mommy?" For the first time the man looked
at Sal with her pert nose, violet eyes, and pixie cut.
"This is all your hair, of course." The man meant to
be sarcastic.

"It is all my hair," said Sal. "But I don't care. You

can have it." Sal could sure be generous, all at the wrong times.

"Now wait a minute. Whose leg you trying to pull here? It would take hundreds of women to grow this amount of hair."

"Naturally," said Sam. "And how much do you want?"

"How much? How MUCH? I — I . . . well . . . it is all alike. But still . . ."

The manager had this sharp, fox-like face and bald head. He wasn't much of an advertisement for his wig manufacturing company. He kept diving into the separate bags of hair and holding up samples, studying it. "The length," he said. "The length is unbelievable. Très jolie." Whatever that meant.

"Sam," said Sal who was beginning to get bored, "Sam, I'm hungry." She tugged at Sam's vest and gave him a pathetic look. You could see Sam wilt. Sal could be very appealing.

"Naturally you're hungry. We haven't eaten and it's well past the time. Come, come, my good man!" Sam was using his booming Admiral's tone. "Do you want the hair or not? We haven't got all day."

"I'll take it. I'll take it. Remarkable. This hair is absolutely remarkable. So fine and yet with body." The bald-headed man danced over to the counter and began writing a check. This bothered me a bit. What in the world would we do with a check?

"My good man," said Sam, "we want cash. And I don't believe I heard the amount you were paying us.

Let us not assume that we automatically accept. After all, this is a country of free enterprise." And Sam kind of glared at the man.

The man choked. He sputtered. Finally he got out some words. "Monsieur," he said, "the price . . . the price is standard in this business. We all pay the same price, no matter where you go. For this quantity . . ." He stopped and looked at Sam. "Naturellement, this could not be from one person's head. What a fantastic idea."

"You've hit on the right word there," I muttered. But the manager wasn't listening to me. He was talking to Sam. And he offered him $350 for the whole batch.

"Yikes," I breathed.

"Good!" said Sam. "We accept. In cash, please."

They didn't have the cash which isn't surprising but they sent out for it. And while we waited the manager tried to pump Sam for his formula, the one for stimulating hair growth. Sam looked blank and fierce all at once which is not easy to do. And he kept saying, "It's all in the blades, you know." Which made me snicker. And certainly didn't make any sense to the manager. Once the money was in hand, Sam swept Sal and me out the door, hailed a cab and took us to a funny little snack place called Chock Full o' Nuts. Whether this described the customers or the food, I never did find out.

Sam wouldn't let us order much. It was getting late in the afternoon and he announced, just like that, that he wanted to take us to the new Lincoln Center. "I think we should try a bit more of the cultural side of New York," he said.

Culture, when mentioned, always makes me feel slightly nauseated. But Sam was somebody I wouldn't dare argue with. So I followed orders. Sal and I ate only a hamburger and glass of milk, neither of which turned out to be chock full of nuts. Then Sam took us back to the hotel and told us to get into our best clothes. Neither of us said "Boo" to the idea. Maybe even culture could be fun with Sam. Though I didn't remember anything very exciting happening at the Guggenheim Museum. Sal was off in the tub sudsing away when I suddenly remembered that Sam had gone off to Ireland to see our parents. "Did you talk to the folks?" I asked Sam.

He was sitting in the chair by the window with his eyes shut. Maybe he was off somewhere. "Folks? Folks? Ah, you mean your parents," said Sam with a funny, nervous jerk. "Impossible to communicate with them. They were in a highly nervous and emotional state. A strange word kept popping into their minds. Let me see. It had to do with you children napping. Strange? Do you take naps, Tryg?"

"Heck!" I almost exploded at the thought. "Sal and I haven't taken naps in years. I guess you made a mistake, Sam."

Sam frowned at me. He didn't like that suggestion. I turned and hurried to get dressed.

7

The Vanishing Americans

We were walking down the hall toward the elevators when I took my first good look at Sal. Up to that time I'd been so shook by her pixie haircut and the way it seemed to change her personality that I simply never bothered to look at all of her. But now I couldn't avoid it. "Yikes!" I gasped it out.

Sam heard. He was sharp, that one. He turned and said, "Something bothering you, Tryg?"

"You could say that," I said. "We've got to go back, Sam. It's all wrong."

"Tut, tut, tut, Tryg. Going out to dinner and the theater can't be *all* wrong."

"But don't you see, Sam. You've got Sal's dress on backward. Girl's sashes don't tie in a big bow on their stomachs. And they almost never zip down the front. That dress is on backward."

Sam stood there shaking his head. "Can't see all this fuss about doing things the usual way. What's so wrong in being different?"

Sal looked down at the full skirt of the red and white

polka-dotted nylon. She looked again. "I like it," she said.

That sister of mine was sure practicing to get slugged. By me. Oh, what was the use. If it was all right with Sam and her why should I worry. I shrugged my shoulders and we all kept going toward the elevators. The big bow bouncing up and down on Sal's stomach kind of led us all on. And the idea made me grin. With such a backward start maybe the evening would be a real dilly. I certainly hoped so. Because pure, undiluted culture sounded dreary.

Naturally, we didn't take off immediately for Lincoln Center. Nope. Sam had some business to do. He insisted on paying for the hotel bill while he still had money. The way Sam spent the stuff, I wasn't about to object. But the cashier did. People just didn't settle their bills in the middle of a stay at a New York hotel. He tried to argue with Sam. Which was a mistake. Sam began to get angry all over again with people person's insistence on the humdrum and usual. And as he got angry, he began to grow, a little at a time. Until he was absolutely huge, at least six feet six inches tall. The cashier grumbled and grouched, but he gave in. I thought him a super-grinch, but even a super-grinch couldn't resist Sam when he was insisting.

Well, the bill was gigantic. Not that I'm used to paying hotel bills, but the size of it made me gasp. Why it was close to $150. I felt worried inside. If the folks didn't come soon the $350 Sam was paid for Sal's hair wouldn't last long. Not with Sam in control. Still, as he had promised, something had come along. And maybe it would again.

When we were finally settled in the cab, Sam leaned across Sal and gave me $25. "To pay you back for your advances those first days," said Sam. Which was generous of him, since Sal and I were the ones doing the eating and sleeping that cost all the money.

The trip across town was a hot one. Because Sal refused to roll down the windows. She didn't want her hair to blow, she said. What a laugh. She didn't fool me a bit. The reason she didn't want the window down was that she wanted to admire herself in the glass. Girls, bah!

I can't say that I was very impressed when we climbed out at Lincoln Center. It was a great mass of concrete with huge buildings rearing up on each side. In the center was a fountain. But what a fountain. Can you imagine a spray of water that looks like a shimmering giant of a feather? That's the way this water was spraying. In case you might get tired of it, the height of the spray kept shifting. Sometimes it went way up, sometimes way down. Made me nervous. Wish whoever was running the dumb thing would make up his mind.

Of course I didn't have long to be nervous because Sam had stopped someone to ask where the opera building was and once he had his directions he strode away with gigantic steps. Well, what kind of steps

would a person six feet six take? Sal and I had to run
to keep up. The elevator operator bowed to us like we
were visiting royalty which I sort of figured we were.
At least you could think of Sam as an ambassador from
another country. Sam had dressed for this evening
out too. Oh, he still had on those tight pants and his
crazy deep-topped boots, but he was wearing a swoopy
coat with tails and a white shirt that actually had ruf-
fles up the front. I think you could call him hand-
some.

The head waiter bowed us over to a table smack
against the railing so we had a great view through the
monstrous plate glass windows that rose up, up, up
to the ceiling of the lobby. When I was handed the
large red menu I knew it was going to be expensive.
And when I saw the prices for the dinner I thought
each customer must be paying for at least half a lamb
or cow. Then I got hold of myself. Sam kept warning us to enjoy each adventure. And I decided to do
just that. Hang the cost.

So I had Mignonette of Beef Marchand de Vin and
Sal got Brochette of Lamb. Sam, of course, had nothing. Do you know what my main course turned out
to be? Beef marching through wine. Whooeee! It
tasted awful. I filled up on the rolls and french fries
and salad. Sal got her lamb on a flaming stick which
was a lot more exciting. Tasted better too. I should
know, because I had to help her clean up her plate.
And we ended the meal with a flourish. I got Crêpe
Suzettes and Sal chose Cherries Jubilee because she's

so crazy about cherries. When they brought the desserts in I thought we were going to set the whole place on fire. Because first they set fire to Sal's ice cream sundae and the next moment they were burning up my crêpes which turned out to be very thin pancakes with some delicious gunk inside. The burning didn't hurt the things a bit. They tasted wonderful.

Both Sal and I were almost staggering when we finally got up from the table. It was a lovely feeling. Except when I thought about the evening. Then I lost some of the lovely glow. A play, we were going to see a play. Ugh! But I didn't open my mouth to Sam about this.

He led us out and away from the opera building pointing out as we went the huge Chagall murals on each side of the lobby. He was — how can I say it — perhaps spouting is the right word, yes, I am sure that spouting explains the way his words were flowing. I suddenly wondered if Sam had swallowed some guide book about Lincoln Center and was giving it back to us word for word. He was like a recording tape. After we crossed the concrete plaza to the theater, Sam went over to the box office to get tickets. You know what he bought, don't you? First row seats. I was a little surprised that they were still available. And when we sat down, I had another wave of surprise. Because you could hardly call us early and yet we were sitting all alone in the first three rows of seats. Frit-frat, was there something wrong with them?

I looked around me curiously. So this was the famous Repertory theater. Looked plain vanilla to me. Oh, the aisles were a little steeper maybe than the usual playhouse, but the stage was exactly where stages usually are, smack across the front. Nothing unusual there. The draperies were fancier maybe, but otherwise they looked like most stage curtains. I was so busy with my own thoughts that I didn't notice a couple slip in and sit down beside Sal. That is, I didn't notice them until the woman started to talk. She was a big bony person with a big voice to match. "I absolutely will not sit here, Stanley. If I've told you once I've told you a dozen times that I would not sit in the first three rows. They're not going to make a mistake and drop me in the basement."

Hey, what a crazy remark. Drop the seats? If my hair wasn't so short it might have stood up in surprise. Obviously, the woman was serious. She was really serious. She stood up, her face the kind of red that faces get when a person is angry. Only Stanley wouldn't let her by. He was standing too. And he was explaining in a very firm, patient way that the seats were only dropped into the basement when the director wished to use a thrust stage. That this play did not call for a thrust stage. That they hadn't used a thrust stage in months. And that she was to stop making a fool of herself.

He might as well have been talking to the wall for all the impression he was making on her. But, he was making an impression on me. A big impression! Imagine a theater in which the seats could be dropped into the basement. What a whing-dinger of an idea. Only it didn't appeal to the woman. She shoved past Stanley and steamed up the aisle. The man followed her very slowly. Some people don't have much of a sense of adventure. The thought of all they were missing made me sigh.

"Remarkable," said Sam. "I find the gadget remarkable."

That comment brought me back to the moment with a jolt. "What gadget are you talking about, Sam?" I asked. As if I didn't know.

"Tut, tut, tut, Tryg, you know precisely what I mean. The lift, the elevator, you know, that lowers the seats into the basement. Truly ingenious."

"Are we going to fall?" asked Sal. All the talk was beginning to worry her.

"Now, children. Don't be ridiculous," said Sam. "Nobody is going to fall. They couldn't. The whole gadget is fantastically engineered."

"How do you know?" I asked.

"Because," said Sam with dignity, "I have examined it." If he thought that remark was going to comfort me, he was mistaken. When Sam got fooling around with people person gadgets anything could happen. But he wasn't paying any attention to my doubting looks. He was leaning across me explaining the whole process to Sal. "They have the front rows on a lift, elevator is your word. You throw a lever and down and down go the seats into the basement. That's about twenty feet down. Another gadget on the floor there propels the seats upward again. Up they go part way and slide into a storage place under the main stage. That stage you see in front of you. Meanwhile the thrust stage slides forward into place. This means that by punching a few buttons, pulling a few levers, someone can turn this conventional type theater into a theater in the round. Well, almost round. Absolutely ingenious. Wouldn't you agree?"

Sal nodded. I nodded. And I bet both of us were thinking the same thought at that moment. What would it feel like to get dropped into the basement even on a slow moving lift? Knowing Sam, it was a real possibility. Sam was still talking. He was telling us lots more facts about the theater. From that guide book he had swallowed, I bet. Things like the theater had 565 spotlights. Sam had to have misread that figure. But even a few hundred less would still be a heap of spotlights. Sam was still talking. Only now he was describing the control board that changed the lights. I found this fascinating. He said that a computer ran the lights. Someone punched a card for each change of lights. These were arranged in proper order and fed into the machine automatically. The only thing the operator did was to control the time of the change. Imagine the excitement if Sam ever got his hands on a gadget like that. The results could be really exciting. When Sam got to talking about the size of the theater and cost and the directors, I tuned him out. That kind of stuff bored me.

The next thing I knew, Sal was asking me the name of the show. "Chalk Circle," I said. "Some dumb kid thing, I suppose."

"To the contrary," said Sam. "If you will read the summary in the theater notes you will see that it is a play of ancient China. Two women both claim to be the mother of the same baby. The judge draws a circle on the ground with chalk . . ." So that's where the title came from. "He puts the baby in the center and lets the baby choose. Each woman takes a hand. They can, if they wish, pull the baby in two which would not, I think, be very happy for the baby. Ah, the play begins."

And he was right. The lights were dimming in the auditorium and coming up on the stage. From Sam's short run-down of the story, I could tell it was going to be a very talky kind of play. I am sorry to say I was right. The lines got longer and longer as the women argued. My eyelids got heavier and heavier. And I fell asleep. But I wasn't the only one. Before I dropped off I could tell from the way Sal's head was bobbing that she was doing some first-class sleeping of her own.

A very strange sound awakened me. It sounded as if hundreds of people had all drawn in their breath at once and then let it out in one huge gasp of surprise. I looked at the stage. And galloping guppies! I was making the same noises myself. "Ahhhhhh," I said.

Because the lights on the stage were carrying on like

crazy. I looked for Sam. He was gone. His seat was empty. Goose pimples began chasing each other up and down my spine. The dimmers went from bright sunlight to half light to deep twilight in the space of a few seconds. Which was mighty confusing to the actors who were one moment bathed in the full power of 565 spotlights and the next were groping their way around the stage in a dusky dimness. I thought the lighting effects were really livening up an awfully dull show. Now the lights on the right side zoomed on. Zoomed off. Next the left side spots flashed on. Flashed off. At the very back of the stage a flickering delicate light swelled to brilliance and was gone. I'll say it was gone. It was completely dark on the stage. And the actors were desperately saying their lines as if nothing unusual were happening. Only they were having a hard time of it. They kept running into each other in the completely dark moments. Why, one almost fell off the stage. Then when the lights zoomed on, they'd find themselves in the wrong spot for the action. Lucky the act ended right then, because the actors were beginning to get to the end of their nonchalance. I know. I know. The show must go on. But it's darn hard when you can't see the stage.

The house lights came on at the proper moment and the audience didn't move. People sat there, stunned. A few people applauded. I don't know whether they were applauding the lights for their mad performance or the actors for their grit in keeping on. Voices began humming around us. Everybody was excited.

Let's face it. I thought it was about the best show I'd ever seen.

Suddenly I realized that Sam was back. And he was wearing this pleased pussycat grin. "Hey, Sam," I said, "That was great."

"Botheration," said Sam. "You noticed?" What a guy. As if anyone could help noticing.

"Do it again, Sam," said Sal. "It was fun."

"True," said Sam. "I really enjoyed it. But the operator of the lights is quite frantic. I think it best not to trouble him again. Enough is enough."

Still Sam kept smiling his pussycat smile and my goose pimples kept right in action. I could hardly wait for the next act to begin, which is not my normal reaction at a play.

This act had a little more action. You could almost feel the tension building on stage. The chalk circle was drawn. The little boy was placed in the center. Then yikes! The stage began to move. It had a revolving stage to change scenery and the stage was revolving. Only it wasn't meant to revolve. Not at this point. The actors suddenly found themselves out in the wings saying their lines and the audience was looking at an empty stage. Different, to say the least. Then back from the wings came the actors and their set and the other one moved away. Pretty bewildering for the actors. They didn't know whether to pick up the lines they were speaking or start over again. But they were game. They kept going. Only some of them seemed to have lost their place in the play. The

speeches didn't jibe, like a zipper that's out of align-
ment. It was screwy. It was great!

And then, galloping guppies! This time it wasn't
the actors who disappeared. It was us. Our
whole row started downward. Very slowly down-

ward like we were on a gigantic elevator. I watched
the dark hole above us where a few moments ago we'd
been sitting. It was edged with light now, almost like a
halo. Gently we touched bottom. I craned my neck
to see what was happening. Twenty feet is quite a
drop. Especially when you watch yourself retreating
from solidness. Sal was gripping my hand so tightly
that I could almost feel her bones rubbing mine.

Then slowly we began to rise. We went right back
up where we had been. Of course, we had been missed.
Some women were screaming. There were a few
others in the rows behind us who had taken the ride
too and they seemed to take a very dim view of such
novel seats. We had hardly rocked back into place
when they scrambled away. As far away as they could
get from their seats. Ushers were dashing about,
doing nothing very useful that I could see. And on the
stage, the actors were shouting out their lines in a frantic way. I'll hand this to them. They were a determined bunch of performers. They had to be.

"Botheration," said Sam beside me. "I must have
pulled the wrong lever."

And he was gone. "Sam?" That was Sal and she
had a little quaver in her voice.

Then hot diggity. The seats went down again. But
this time only Sal and I were riding them. No. Sam
was back. His hand grabbed mine. Our feet were
hanging out into space which is an eerie feeling. Especially when it's so dark that you can't see exactly

where you are. We bounced gently on the bottom and started up. But with a difference. The rows of seats stopped this time partway up and began moving forward. We were going under the stage. And from where we were it sure sounded as if there were a heck of a lot of action on that stage above us. I could dimly see a mass of floor moving into position where once our seats had been. The stage must be thrusting forward into position. Hey, Sam must have found the right levers.

Then I heard these funny gasping sounds. That was Sal. She was scared. So scared she couldn't get out any words. Up above I got a glimpse of people's faces staring down through the last open bit of space. Then even they were gone. The floor was solidly in place. And yikes! It was dark down there. A voice at my side said, "Hold on to me, Tryg. Take Sal's hand. We'd better get out of here."

It sounded like Sam. It had to be Sam. Luckily it was Sam.

I did what I was told. And I don't know how Sam managed. But why ask. It was too fabulous to question. We floated through the dark until we came to a tunnel, a tunnel that was going up. Once we got there, our feet made contact with the ground. Sam led and we moved up and out with Sam saying things like, "I wonder if I got the stage in the right place. Marvelous things these levers. Oh, what joy, so many buttons." Good old Sam. And even as I was thinking this thought, we came right out into the audience. We must have been using one of the tunnels the actors used to get to the thrust stage.

What a madhouse the theater was. People were jammed up against the stage as if they were going to force it back into its storage place by their own push. Actors were hanging over the edge, looking . . . looking. I don't know what they expected to see, but they sure had a good view of the floor. Some women were screaming which added a bit to the excitement. Others were yelling at nobody in particular to "DO SOMETHING." How strange that none of them realized what fun it might be riding those seats. Grownups can be funny.

Sam was shoved this way and that. His toes were stepped on. His stomach was rammed with a variety of elbows. And suddenly he said, "Come, come, children. Let us leave. I fear the play is over for tonight."

So we left. It was a struggle since we seemed to be the only people interested in going up the aisle and getting out. When we reached the door, I heard loud scrunching kinds of sounds behind us that could only mean the stage was moving backward. It was. I wanted to wait and see the reaction when they raised up the seats and we were missing. But Sam was in no mood for delay. I had to run to catch up with him and Sal.

As we rode back to the Manor House Sal said, "Sam. I like going to plays with you, Sam."

That was a reasonable statement. I thought about

it a minute. I had to agree that Sam's way of seeing a play sure beat the usual variety. I wasn't too sure, though, about its increasing our "culture." Sam was very silent. Thinking, I guess. Then he spoke. "It amazes me that adults in your world are so rigid in their thinking — non-adjustable. I get the feeling that they detest variety or change."

I snorted. Sal giggled. What a guy. That poor audience, and the actors too, had had enough variety to last them for years. I bet nobody forgot that performance of *The Chalk Circle* ever. And then we were at the hotel and Sam was fumbling around to pay the cab driver. I glanced idly at a newspaper lying on a stand. I hadn't seen a newspaper for days. The headline had something about a kidnapping in it. I wondered who had been kidnapped now. That's a mean kind of crime. And funny, but as we moved toward the elevators I felt as if my memory was nudging my brain trying to surface with an idea. But it never did get through.

It wasn't until Sam had left for the night and Sal was breathing that first, deep, even kind of breathing that comes in sleep, that memory caught up with my thinking. Sam had said something this morning about our folks worrying about our napping. Which was, of course, ridiculous. But supposing the word that had kept coming into their minds had been kidnapping? Sam, being a fairy godfather, wouldn't know that word. The whole thing was so wild it was actually possible. Still, I had cabled my parents that we

were safe. They couldn't possibly think we were kidnapped. But Sam says people persons can get awfully
confused. It all has to do with their non-adjustabil-
ity. Which was the crazy thought I fell asleep on.

8

Baseball, Baseball, Who's Got the Baseball?

THE NEXT DAY did not begin as the other days had. First off, Sam was late. When Sal and I woke up, there was no Sam sitting in the armchair by the window or even walking under my feet. The aloneness scared me a bit. But once I'd brushed my teeth and pulled on my clothes, I felt braver. If Sam could order breakfast, I guess I could too. So I called room service and when the voice asked what I would like my throat felt paralyzed. What should I order? Then I had a useful thought. "Please bring up the same breakfast to room 4007 that you did yesterday," I said.

First there was a silence. Then the voice said, "The same breakfast. Could you be more definite, please."

"No, I can't," I said. "I thought you'd have a record or something." At which point I ran out of braveness and ideas. So I hung up.

But they must have had a record someplace. Because they brought up the same wonderful breakfast though they sure took their time about it. And Sal and I had finished and were looking out the window wondering what to do next when there was Sam. Behind us. A smallish Sam again, about three feet high. He sure did have trouble with the size formula.

"Ah," said Sam. "You are ready? Good! Good!" And he beamed at us.

"Where have you been, Sam?" asked Sal. You couldn't say she wasn't direct.

"Now that's an interesting question. Because I have been to a liquor store."

"Oh, no, Sam," I said. "You aren't taking up drinking."

Sam stared at me for a moment. Then he started laughing. He got to laughing so hard that he had to sit down which wasn't easy since he was so tiny. But he made it. Finally he spoke. "I bought a case of champagne, imported, and sent it to the theater. Plus a floral offering for each of the ladies in the performance. I felt we should make amends. The paper says the performance was ruined."

"Oh no it wasn't, Sam," said Sal. "It was awfully dull until you took over."

"It was great, Sam," I added and I meant it.

"Why, thank you both," said Sam. "But you see, those involved felt some gremlins had slipped in and absolutely destroyed the show. I couldn't let the gremlins take the blame, could I? So I sent the peace offerings. Oh, by the way, Tryg. I do hope you have that twenty-five dollars. I find myself a little short. Peace offerings come high."

"Oh, Sam, you didn't," I said.

But I could tell. He not only could, he had. What a fairy godfather!

"We won't get far on twenty-five dollars," I said glumly. "Not the way you throw money around, Sam."

"Tut, tut, tut! Don't be a spoilsport, Tryg. We'll economize. I know exactly what that word means. You'll see. Today I suggest we go and see a baseball game. I had the Mets in mind."

"I'd rather see the Yankees," I said.

"The Yankees aren't playing here today," said Sam. That sure settled the matter.

Sal was unenthusiastic over the whole proposition. But Sam told her that a person should try everything. How in the world could she really know whether she liked baseball or not if she never tried it?

"I've seen it on TV," said Sal. "Baseball is dull!"

"Aw come on, Sal. How could it be dull with Sam?" Those words popped out without my even thinking. Well, after all, everything else had been that way, so why not baseball? A guy has a right to hope, hasn't he. Sal relaxed. She even smiled. "Okay, Sam, let's go," she said.

So we went. In the elevator I glanced at Sam. Yikes! I'd forgotten about his size. Sam was still pretty small. And I said so.

"Botheration," said Sam. "People persons do keep harping on a man being a certain size. No imagination." For a moment I thought Sam was going to launch on a lecture. But he didn't. "I have no way to judge size, Tryg. I'll start the growing formula. You watch and tell me when to stop."

Sal watched. I watched. And we dropped downward in the elevator. Sam was growing upward in little spurts. I stepped backward to get a better look and neatly leaned against the panel of buttons. Which made us stop at the next floor. And the next. In fact I was so distracted by my foolish mistake that I forgot Sam until I heard this surprised, "Ooooohwoowow." I looked. Frit-frat! Sam's head was against the ceiling of the elevator.

"Stop! Stop!" I yowled. As if he didn't already know.

Sal stood there, her hands cupped over her mouth, giggling.

If Sam had been surprising in the short version he was overwhelming in the super-giant size. A man eight feet four inches high is a lot of man. But top that off with Sam's violent red fringe on his head and the little red beard and you have something startling. Flash went the light over the door and 35 showed up. Stop went the elevator. Whoosh went the doors. A man standing outside, started in, stopped in shock, and stared. He backed up. The door shut. We dropped downward. I pushed the *EMERGENCY* button. If this wasn't an emergency what would you call it? Sam was glowering at me. "I thought," he said, "that you were going to tell me when to stop?"

I didn't argue the point. "Better shrink," I told Sam.

"And hurry. Because we might get help quicker than we want."

"Tryg," said Sam, "you are obviously very ignorant about our formulas. I cannot use the shrinking formula on top of the growing formula here in your land. So I shall have to step back to my world and meet you in the lobby."

One thing about Sam. He never gave you long to think about something. Just like that, he was gone. I punched the button for the main floor and we started down again. When the door opened there was a mechanic standing there waiting. "Oh," he said disgustedly, "it was only some kids fooling around."

I swallowed hard, a little frightened, because he looked mighty angry. And right then the man from the thirty-fifth floor who had seen Sam in all his glorious size stepped up and insisted . . . "No, no! There was a giant in that elevator." Sal and I gave him this wide-eyed stare. "At least I think there was," he said kind of weakly.

Quick as quick I steered Sal toward the lobby door. And sure enough, standing outside was Sam. Quite a proper size now. He signaled for a cab. I started to argue about economy, but Sam was in no mood for argument. So we rode that cab all the way out to Flushing Meadow. I was lucky the ball park wasn't in the next state. Once at Shea Stadium I was shocked to find the big hole that ride had put in my funds. I tried repeating to myself, "Enjoy it! Enjoy it!" But I managed to get beside Sam at the ticket window and say, "Economy, Sam — remember?"

"Of course. Of course," he said testily. Seems that grown-ups, no matter what their land, don't want kids telling them their business. I was lucky this time because there were no expensive seats left. We ended up in the bleachers which was okay with me. Naturally, we had to hike about a mile to get to the right spot. Then we had a jolly time finding our seats. I bet we piled past about a million legs and knees before we could sit down. Only there was mighty little space to sit down in. Everybody had spread out into the empty seats. Well, the three of us sat down in a solid lump — kind of one, two, three. And then we began wiggling and shoving and squeezing to get some space back. Otherwise we couldn't have kept breathing.

The game began. So did Sal's complaints. I admit that the diamond was so far away that the players looked like dolls, but what can you expect of the poorest seats? I thought we were lucky to still be in the ball park. Then right on the tail of her complaints, Sal began asking stupid questions. "Where's the diamond?"

I told her. And she asked why it was called that when it didn't even sparkle. I let that remark go by. "Who's the man with the funny dohickus on his chest?"

"The umpire," I said.

"Why does he jump around like that, holding up first one arm and then the other?"

Questions, questions, questions. Who can enjoy a game when he's being swamped with questions? So I got smart. I suggested she have an ice cream bar. Maybe that would keep her quiet for a while. And it did. It worked fine. Except that once she started eating, Sal kept right on. She got a hot dog and then some popcorn and some cotton candy. The last occupied her the longest. But I was getting worried. My money was rushing away. I complained to Sam that with Sal's eating we might have to walk back to the hotel. So Sam refused to buy Sal anything more. Which didn't increase her good humor.

At the seventh inning stretch, Sal began whining about leaving. The way the game was going we probably wouldn't miss much. The Mets were playing their usual "hard luck" kind of ball. Nothing they did came out right. The score was five to two in favor of the Cardinals. Sam himself admitted at this point that he couldn't understand the game. He felt the players did an awful lot of standing around. And I agreed that this didn't make the game awfully exciting. But this was the usual way of baseball.

The minute I used that word "usual" I had this funny feeling. Because saying anything was usual to Sam was like waving red cloth at a bull. Still, what could he do at a baseball game? Obviously, nothing, because the game went up to the ninth inning in the same old way that baseball games usually go. Just about then, Sal began complaining again. This time she was whining that she couldn't see the ball.

I really snapped at her. I guess I was feeling the heat myself. "You can't see it, dummy, because the ball moves fast and it's small."

"H'mmmm," said Sam and rubbed his nose very hard as if it were itching.

The pitcher unwound and let fly with a fast curved ball. The umpire yelled, "Strike!" The batter stood

there staring. The catcher was hopping around looking for something. Galloping guppies! They were looking for the ball. Which was not surprising. Because Sal was holding it in her lap. We both sat there staring at it open-mouthed and Sam had a pleased little grin on his face. But down on the diamond a regular rhubarb was brewing with all the players shouting and yelling and nobody listening at all. Mainly everybody was demanding that "somebody" produce the ball.

The umpire gave up and signaled for another ball and the game moved on. The Cardinal pitcher was so unnerved by the ruckus that he walked the Met batter. So now the Mets had one man on base. The next player gave the ball a wallop and made it safely to first. The man on first beat the throw to second. And for the first time in the game the Mets had two men on base and no outs. Then Sam decided that the game was slowing down. On the next pitch, the ball disappeared as it was flying toward the batter. I suppose to be fair about it the umpire called this missing pitch a "ball," which nobody took calmly. The fans were screaming advice, the catcher and umpire looked as if they were going to get in a fight, the batter wanted to get started playing. It was absolutely delicious. Sal and I sat there with idiotic smiles on our faces, because Sal now had two balls in her lap. This was a great game. Not exactly baseball, but great just the same.

The next pitch was a very ordinary one. The catcher even caught it. The umpire yelled "Strike!"

The catcher dropped the ball. And it vanished. Sal now had three balls in her lap. And the situation on the diamond was getting ridiculous. The umpire was accusing the catcher of hiding the ball. The batter was arguing that he must have hit a homer. The pitcher and the coaches, well, just about everybody was trying to get into the act. And in the stands people were standing up and shouting and pushing. Sal and I climbed up on the seats so we could see.

At which moment, Sam decided to return a ball. He was awfully accommodating. Sal suddenly had only two balls and a very startled pitcher was clutching the other in his hand. He stared at his mitt, baffled, confused. He'd never even held up his glove and yet there was the ball. People were yelling, "Play ball!"

The pitcher wound up and let go. The ball bobbled toward the batter. That's the only way I can describe its action. It bounced, it zigged, it skittered a bit, all in fantastic slow motion. Finally it made a lurch across the plate and sank in the catcher's mitt. And that catcher took a death grip on it. He was going to hold on to it this time, that's for sure. The batter was shouting that the pitch was illegal. The coaches were insisting that a strike be called. The umpire said nothing. He simply didn't know what to call it, except maybe crazy. And the ball park was one mighty shriek of voices. Everybody was shouting something, either to the people next to him or to the players. A few even launched fists at neighbors who disagreed.

The catcher finally heaved the ball back to the
pitcher. The pitcher stood there waiting, for a signal
I suppose. And then the ball was gone. Sal had her
three balls back again. I took one to help her out. The
pitcher turned and walked off the field. He acted
dazed. They sent in another man and another ball and
the game went on. This time the catcher didn't bother
to signal the pitch. He was resigned to madness.
Zoom, the ball whipped toward the batter at a wild
speed. The bat connected. The ball took off. But not
properly at all. It began to bounce, gigantic bounces
as if a giant were playing one, two, three o'leary. Each
time the ball neared an infielder or baseman it went
high into the air way above his head. So the fielders
were running hither and yon, skidding this way and
that, trying to catch up with the ball. Around and
around the field bounced the ball. The stands were in
an uproar. And the Mets were busy running the bases
like crazy men. The scoreboard ticked off three runs.
The game was tied five all.

Sam suggested we should leave. It looked as if a
first-class riot were about to break out. They were still
trying to play ball down on the diamond. I got a
glimpse of another pitch. The bat connected. Yikes!
I had a ball in my other hand. Sam had snagged a fly
ball. People were all very quiet now, staring into the
sky, shading their eyes to see better. But nobody saw
the ball. The batter whirled around the bases. He had
just passed third when we shoved our way up to the
exit. Sam said to me very quietly, "Let's give some of

those balls back, children. It's always bad to be greedy."

I felt as if strong little fingers grabbed the two balls in my hands. They were gone. One of Sal's was missing too. And out on the field the watchers spotted a high soaring ball. No, not one ball! There were three balls gracefully floating down. The rightfielder, the leftfielder and the shortstop each caught one. And as good ballplayers do, they all snapped their balls to the catcher. Well, he caught the first one all right and was going to tag the Met runner when bongo!

The second ball whizzed in and hit his right shoulder. And the third ball smashed into his rump.

The roar from the crowd was fantastic as the scoreboard tallied a run for the Mets. People were pounding each other madly. The players on the field were arguing about the balls. And just about everyone in the stands decided to get down onto the field. How exciting. What a mad, wonderful game. But Sam could be single-minded. He kept nudging us toward the gate. Since nobody else seemed interested in leaving, we had no trouble in getting out.

Sam walked us toward the subway station. He kept muttering things about "Variety — how life must always have variety. How we should never settle for the usual, the ordinary." Stuff like that.

Behind us we could hear sirens. Sounded like dozens of sirens were zeroing in on Shea Stadium. Obviously Sam's type of variety had started something exciting. As we walked along I got to wondering how the sports writers were going to describe this game. And would they credit the Mets with a win? Gosh, being with Sam was fun. Everybody should have a fairy godfather! Say, maybe they do.

9

Crazy With the Heat?

OUR FINALLY FINDING the subway station and a train had nothing to do with Sam's magic. He was simply so big that when he stopped this scrawny-looking young man and asked for directions, the fellow not only told us how to get there, but walked right along with us for a block or two to be sure we wouldn't miss it.

Once at the station, we got on a train and were off with a jolt and roar. Out in Flushing Meadow the subway isn't a subway exactly. Because it runs on top of the ground which made it seem somewhat cooler if anything could be cool on such a sizzling day. Eventually, of course, it dipped back under the dirt which was absolutely awful. The sun had been giving us a first-class demonstration all day long of how hot it could make New York. And down in the dark tunnels where the trains run, it was suffocating. The fan blades kept turning the air around, but who likes getting hit in the face by hot air. Nobody talked. Women mopped at their faces and pushed back limp-looking hair. Most of the men had their jackets off and sleeves rolled. And they looked plenty hot too.

"Whooo!" sighed Sal.

She had reason for that sigh, jammed in as she was between Sam and me on one of those long benches. I couldn't rouse enough energy to comment. Sam sat there with his eyes shut. I thought he must be asleep. And onward we rode. All the sounds of the train seemed extra loud. Maybe heat does that. "The tropics," said Sam suddenly. "That's what it reminds me of. The tropics."

So he hadn't been sleeping. Just thinking. "Reminds me of the Tunnel of Love at our amusement park." I shouted this. I had to. The noises were that intense.

"Tunnel of Love?" Sam bellowed back at me. Those words came out so loud and strong that some of the people standing and clinging to straps almost went over backward.

"That's what they call it," I said, not quite so loudly.

Frit-frat! If there'd been a hole I'd have crawled into it. People were staring. Some even snickered. But I had to explain the thing to Sam. For some crazy reason it seemed important. "The Tunnel of Love is like a jungle ride. It's supposed to be scary, see? The lights go off and weird things come lurching at you like skeletons or a giant ape or maybe a tiger. And always they've got these giant crocodiles with great, wide, snapping jaws. Just make-believe, but it's great. Really great!"

"This make-believe," said Sam, "why do they do this?"

Galloping guppies! What a dumb thing to have to explain. But being plain stupid, I tried. "People like to be scared. See?" Sam looked doubtful. "But they do," I argued. "Fellows take their girl friends on the ride and the girls pretend to be scared. They grab the boy, I think." Oh, man! This was embarrassing. "I think the boy may give her a hug or squeeze or even start smooching."

"Smooching? What is this smooching?" asked Sam.

I was getting redder. And it wasn't all the heat. People were staring at Sam and me like everything. "Smooching is kissing," I said.

Sam sat there, very quietly as if he were digesting the idea. "They hug and smooch," he said. "That I like. Hugging and kissing is very nice."

"Aw, Sam." I blushed so red that my face color was way out ahead of my hair color for redness. I tried to avoid looking at the people in front of us hanging on straps and staring. My eyes focused on the upside-down part of a newspaper. The man in front of me was clutching a big brown paper sack and this newspaper. Reading words that are upside down is sure a challenge. I figured out that the kidnapping was still big news. Two kids yet. That kidnapper was ambitious snatching two at once. But why take two kids?

And right as I was puzzling through this thought

and before I could read more, I heard a bunch of funny squeaks. It was Sal. I looked at her and she looked strange. Her face was kind of petrified. Nothing was moving. Her eyes were wide and staring. Her mouth hung at half-mast.

I had to crane my neck around the bag of groceries to see at all. And I saw plenty. Women's purses, assorted colored fabrics in dresses and suits and a teensy bit of window ahead. Galloping guppies! A monkey! No! A huge ape had a grip on that window on the outside. He was clutching it broadside. And what mean eyes he had. They really glared at us. I heard a woman shriek, "Look at that! Look at that!"

What a holler. Everyone looked all right. But most

of them looked at her, so they missed the ape. We roared into a station. Remember that New York subway game — the people on the inside rush to get out and those on the outside rush to get in? It makes each stop interesting. You can bet with yourself whether the "inners" or "outers" will make the break through first. This time those outside won out. But we did get our passengers unloaded at last and away the train went down the track. Being an express, we roared along for blocks and blocks, maybe miles without a stop.

And then suddenly the lights in the train went out. There were assorted squeals, squeaks, shrieks, and grunts. But those sounds were quiet compared to the next ones. With it so dark on the inside of the train, the tunnel outside looked very bright. But it was a strange kind of brightness. Luminous and dark all at once. I could hear a man, probably the policeman — there's a policeman on every subway train, you know — this voice was demanding to know, "What's going on here?"

And right then I saw them — three tigers racing the train. They were moving at a terrific speed. Their eyes glittered in a frightening way. They were going to attack. Yikes! They were going to attack the train. The lights came on. The tigers were gone. Sam had a pleased expression on his face. Most of the passengers sat there mopping at their faces. Perspiring, gasping for breath. I wonder if it was all from the heat. Surely some had seen what I had seen. Sal had a grip on my arm like she thought she was drowning. I glanced at her. And she looked terrified, but excited. How wonderful.

The policeman shoved his way past our seat as he headed toward the motorman's cubbyhole up ahead. Then the lights went out again. This time you couldn't miss the creature outside. It was a skeleton. The darnedest skeleton I had ever seen. Its bones were glistening like neon tubes. Its eye sockets were great red holes. And it was dancing like a bunch of bones gone mad. A woman spotted it and began to scream. There is nothing scarier when you're in the dark than a good, high-pitched, healthy scream. I think at first that some people thought the poor soul was having a heat stroke. Or possibly just going nuts from the heat. People always try to find a nice, simple answer for a complicated event. The woman screamed on. Others saw the skeleton and joined in the shrieking chorus. The sound was deafening. Now people began shoving, stumbling around. I don't know where they were going. The places to go are rather limited when you're roaring down a tunnel at sixty miles an hour.

The lights came on. The policeman was advancing on us waving a gun. He looked about as scared as any man I've ever seen. But then how often does one have an animated skeleton banging around at the windows on a hot day in July. He was struggling to say something. Nobody was listening. Sam seemed to be saying something to me. But I couldn't hear his words. We roared into a station. And what a stampede there

was to get out. There was no question who'd win the
game this time. The "inners" were so determined to
get out that those on the platform had to give way.
The policeman ran up and down the platform waving
his pistol. Looked as if he might take a pot shot at the
roof of the train. But he didn't. Last I saw of him, he
was getting on the rear car of the train. And we
roared away from the station.

Now, the man standing in front of me with the groceries had never budged during all the action. He had
just stood there, bored, as if he was accustomed to the
lights going on and off, and women screaming and policemen charging up and down the aisles. But all of a
sudden he let out a strange sound. "Hyenas! HY-
ENAS!" he shouted.

I had to bend myself almost into a pretzel to see
what that fellow must be seeing. Boy! I was sure
close to the action. Because right beside the window
there were hyenas running like crazy. And silently,
swiftly, deadly, three tigers were pursuing them. Instead of looking outside, the passengers were all staring at the shouting madman in front of me. And he
kept shouting the same thing. "Hyenas, hyenas."

I saw one of the tigers make a fantastic leap. A
hyena went down. Then they were all gone.

"Hyenas, hy . . . eeenas," said the man running
out of steam. "I think." He added this almost apologetically.

All around us people were murmuring, commenting
as they always do when something unusual happens.

More handkerchiefs blossomed out and more people mopped at their faces.

Sam, I noticed, had a very puzzled expression on his face. I looked where he was looking and yikes! He was looking at this young couple sitting across from us. Talk about being locked in each other's eyes. They hadn't even noticed all the hollering and action going on. Hey! Was Sam trying for some "smooching"? So far he'd gotten a variety of reactions but he'd certainly not attained that one. Oh, oh! Here came the policeman again. He was stomping down the aisle with the stolid, determined stride of a very befuddled man.

Oops! The lights went out again. This time we really got a taste of Sam's varieties. First off, the train slammed to a stop. Now in the dark, a stop is murder. I got the hyena man, groceries and all, in my lap. Sam drew a couple of women and Sal was almost smashed flat by a great mountain of a woman. All of which brought on another chorus of screaming. But things didn't get better. Nope, they got worse. Because outside, in the eerie light we could see the biggest, longest crocodile I ever have seen, slithering along beside the train. I bet it was twenty feet long at least. No wonder we had stopped with a jerk. If the motorman hadn't stopped, that great beast would have derailed the train. Since this line has an interlocking kind of safety system, I knew that all down the line trains were stopping. Which was an exciting thought.

The policeman spotted the crocodile. And he let

out a whoop that you could hear over everything else. Then he let loose with a spectacular series of words. The young couple had stopped looking at each other. Mainly because they were in a heap on the floor. Looked as if Sam had still missed on the "smooching." The policeman stepped over these kids, grabbed off his shoe and broke out the window like in a spy movie. And galloping guppies! Next thing we knew he was emptying his pistol at the crocodile. Which didn't bother it one bit. It kept right on slithering along as if nothing was happening. What with the gunfire and the screaming and the darkness I was beginning to hatch a great crop of goose pimples. Holy cow! It was really exciting.

The man in my lap began cursing. Then everybody made a mass effort to get to the doors and through them. But before they could, the train started off with a jiggle and a juggle. And zap! zap! down the tracks we went. Once in the next station people scrambled out of the train as if they were one step ahead of a nightmare. Most of them were screeching at the waiting passengers, things about tigers and crocodiles. But mainly they were hollering for help. None of this made much sense to those on the platform. I bet they thought the whole bunch had gone crazy with the heat. The train moved on. There were only a few people left. And they were mopping at their faces like the others had done. A strange quiet settled down. The young couple had charged off at the last station. Which was pretty disappointing because

we'd never get to see now the other wonders that
Sam might dream up for a Tunnel of Love. My friend
of the grocery bag had left too. But he'd left the groceries smack in my lap.

"Amazing," said Sam, very thoughtfully. "Amazing. I don't understand what happened to the fun and
enjoyment and smooching. I do believe that I don't
understand people persons at all."

"Sam, you wonderful nut," I said. I meant it too.
"Don't you see? This was too unexpected and real. At
an amusement park you know it's make-believe."

"Ah so!" said Sam. "I do not believe that people
persons like variety. They worship the usual. They
detest the unusual. Very dull."

"Not with you, Sam," I said.

Sam smiled. He liked to be appreciated. Sal snug-
gled up to him. "I love you, Sam," she said.

"Tut, tut, tut," said Sam. It was the only time I ever
saw Sam embarrassed. He was quite a guy. "Come,
we'll get off here. I seem to have lost track of exactly
where we are."

So we got off. Climbing up the stairs was like rising
out of a steam bath. The air outside wasn't awfully
cool, but it was sheer heaven compared to the air below. We trudged along with Sam. I was still hauling
the sack of groceries. Which turned out to be a lucky
thing. Because the sack was filled with food from a
delicatessen. When you're as broke as we were, it was
nice to have supper provided and free at that. We had
two kinds of cheese and potato salad and baked beans

and rye bread and cold cuts and dill pickles. We didn't have plates or knives and forks, so Sam suggested we try experimenting with sandwiches. Baked beans and potato salad sure are different sandwich fillings. Not good, but different.

I was settling back with that satisfied feeling that comes when your stomach is comfortably full and I happened to look across at Sal. There she was, a piece of sandwich still clutched in her hand, her head back against the chair, her eyes shut tight. Sal was sound asleep. Sam gently shook her into her night things. I couldn't pin down the reason for my feeling, but I sensed a strange urgency about Sam's actions tonight. He was troubled. Only I was too tired to ask what was wrong. And I doubt if even a fairy godfather would bother to tell a kid. Besides, something was bound to turn up.

I fell into my pajamas, tumbled into bed and before I could finish saying, "Good night, Sam," he was gone.

10

The All-American Ice

It WAS HARD waking up the next morning. Not that the dreams I had at night could possibly hold a patch on the adventures Sal and I were having daytimes. But I was tired. Excitement and happiness can be very tiring. And there you are.

It was almost noon before I could get my eyelids to separate permanently into that state called "being awake." Every now and then I'd flip them open for a moment. I had the feeling that somebody was sitting in the chair by the window. Good! Sam must be back.

And sure enough, when I finally groaned out of bed, Sam's voice said, "Botheration and bubble gum! I thought you two were planning to sleep the whole day away."

I hate talking first thing in the morning. So I nodded. I managed to grind out "good morning," which came out a jumble of grumpy sounds. Sal was struggling back from the bathroom and since she still doesn't talk too much, I didn't even bother speaking to her. I was brushing my teeth when I heard Sam talking to somebody. Must be the waiter with our breakfast. Funny, but the waiter sounded strange. His voice was trembling.

"I need some money, Tryg." That was Sam.

"I haven't got any," I yelled back through the door.

"Botheration," said Sam. I heard the waiter leave so Sam must have thought of something.

I trudged back like a zombie to the bedroom. And galloping guppies! I came to with a jolt. Now I knew why the waiter sounded dazed. Sam was shrinking. He was only twenty-four inches high by now. "Sam, Sam, watch it. You're disappearing."

"Tut, tut, tut," said Sam. "I do keep forgetting to use the 'hold' formula. It's such a nuisance. They're taking the fun out of magic with all their science."

Sam sounded grumpy. So I kept quiet and so did Sal. We did the logical thing at that moment. We ate breakfast. And when we had finished I looked toward the armchair. There was Sam. But a full-sized Sam now. And he still looked unhappy. That puzzled me. I couldn't think of a thing that Sal and I might have done to bring this on. "Sam?"

Sam stopped staring out the window. "Are you finished, children?" he asked. "I never like telling bad news to anyone with an empty stomach."

How's that for the beginning of a story? My heart sank. "I know we're out of money, Sam," I said quicklike, "but I bet something will turn up."

"Oh, that? That's nothing," said Sam. "I agree. Something will turn up. But this other. It's inefficiency. That's what it is."

Sam had never seemed very excited about efficiency before. Or had he? I didn't ask. Because he had this long, sad look on his face. Oh, boy! here it came. The worst.

"I've lost your parents," said Sam.

"Lost our parents?" Sal and I chorused that together.

"Aw, Sam, don't worry," I said. "They'll turn up. You'll see."

The words popped out of me. I hadn't even realized I was going to say them. Sam stared at me a moment. Then his face began to crack up. I don't mean he was falling apart. But the serious lines vanished and Sam was laughing. When Sam laughed, you couldn't help yourself. You had to laugh too. So we did. We laughed and hollered until our insides ached. And though we didn't know exactly why, we all felt better. "Thanks, Tryg," said Sam. "I needed that laugh. Clears the cobwebs in the brain. Laughter does. Now let me tell you what happened. I had an apprentice godfather on the job in Ireland, keeping track of your folks. We train godfathers in my land this way. And it gave me the chance to spend the day with you. I knew he was skittish. He's got a poor record. And he did it again. He got to fooling around riding a light wave. Well, between one ride and another, your parents vanished from Ireland. And we can find no trace of them."

"Oh, oh," I said. "They'll be worried if we don't meet them."

"But where to meet them?" said Sam. "That's the question."

"Hic, hic," said Sal. Now Sal wasn't drunk. She simply gets the hiccups when she laughs too hard. And we certainly had had a binge of laughing. So Sal went off to the bathroom to get a drink. It took her so long I began to wonder if she had drowned. "Sam, help, Sam, the ice machine." That was Sal.

Oh boy, that ice machine is a twentieth-century gadget that I really dig. Each bathroom in this hotel had one. It was a small machine and it kept filling the tray inside the little box set in the wall until the box was full. Then it automatically shut off. Pretty neat, eh? Sam started off toward the bathroom, rubbing the bump on his nose, thoughtful-like. And little shivers started somewhere at the base of my neck. I had goose pimples on goose pimples and I didn't know why.

Sam was gone for some time. Which I expected. If there is one thing Sam loves, it's people person gadgets. When he came out, he announced that it was fixed. Next he told us to stay in the room until he got back. He wanted to go and check on our parents' whereabouts for himself. "Here are some newspapers to look at," he said. And presto! He was gone.

I looked down at the papers and frit-frat! I had

only the front pages. I took another look. And I had this crazy need to clap my hands. It was nuts. But sometimes excitement has to get out of you some way. Because right there on the front page of that New York newspaper was a picture of Sal walking upside down across the ceiling. Not that anybody else would recognize her as Sal. But having been there, I couldn't miss. In the other paper there was a picture of the ferry trying to land. The fireboat was spraying it toward shore on a great plume of water. Why there was even a picture of the Admiral and his godchildren, which was Sal and me. But somehow the thing was a bit blurred. Sal's face was hidden on Sam's shoulder and I was behind him in his shadow. Still, how often does a guy make the front page of a newspaper twice in one week. I glanced at the date lines. Why heck! These papers were days old. Sam must have found them in a trash can. Big deal!

Naturally Sal had to have a look. And then we started playing that fun game of "remember when." We had lots to remember on this trip to New York. In fact we were so busy remembering that I couldn't connect the knocking sounds with the words we were saying. But I came back in a hurry. Of course. The waiter had come to pick up the dirty dishes. I started down the short hall leading to the outside door and yikes! The sight in the bathroom stopped me cold. Because that ice machine was sure working overtime. It was spilling out ice cubes as if the whole bathroom was one huge box that had to be filled. And man!

That little machine was going to fill it or bust. I bet there were about a foot of cubes on the floor already. But here's a strange thing. They weren't ordinary cubes at all. These cubes were red and white and blue.

The knocking grew louder. "Just a minute, just a minute," I shouted. Then I called to Sal, "Hey, open the door, will you, Sal?"

I could hear her moving toward me. Protesting, grumbling, but coming. I made a leap into the bathroom and onto the cubes. What a jolt! I've never tried walking on eggs, but I bet walking on ice cubes comes close to the feeling. It was wild. The cubes tilted, changed positions, shifted again. I was teetering and stumbling at the same time. But I had to get the bathroom door shut. No waiter was going to be quiet about a bathroom filled with ice cubes. I knew he'd go and spoil all the fun. I lost my balance, fell against the door and whamo! Slammed it shut. But I was slammed down on the floor, face first. Hey! What a wild accident to be lying flat on colored ice cubes on the fortieth floor of a New York hotel. The thought made me giggle madly. But not for long. I was giggling ice down my neck. Brrrr.

I could hear the sounds of the waiter trundling the cart out. The door shut. "Hey, Sal," I called. "Come here, quick."

"I don't want to," said Sal. She sounded cross.

"Yes, you do. Yes, you do," I shouted. "Come on in. The ice is fine."

That last puzzled her. And Sal is curious. I heard her twisting the handle on the door. It turned, but the door stayed shut. Then I saw why. Of course. The machine behind me was tumbling the cubes out like crazy and there was such a pile against the door that Sal couldn't get it open. Meaning to be helpful, I grabbed the handle on my side and pulled as hard as I could. With my pulling and Sal's pushing, we got action. The door opened with a whoosh and Sal flipped in, airborne for a moment. Then down she went, crunch, smunch against the carpet of ice. I waited for shrieks, eyes shut. Sal never has been partial to having her face washed with snow. And an ice bath had to be worse. But no shrieks came. I opened my eyes and felt slightly panicked. She was lying so quietly. Galloping guppies! She might be dead.

I scrunched down on the ice to get a better look. Aw, she wasn't dead at all. Not even hurt. That dumb kid was eating the ice cubes. And she had this completely happy look on her face like a bear with a pot full of honey. Naturally I thought I'd better sample an ice cube or two myself. And you know something. She was right. You've never tasted stuff like those cubes. The red ones were cherry flavored, a sharp, sour cherry that made your tongue tingle. I tried a white cube next, expecting vanilla. But I sure was wrong. The flavor was pineapple and lemon sort of tart and sweet at once. I hesitated at the blue colored ones. I had a fleeting idea that they might taste like ink and that's not my favorite taste. But you've got

to be venturesome. At least Sam's always urging us to try the unusual. So I bit in bravely. What in heck was it? Blueberries? No, no! Not blueberries — blue grapes.

The bathroom was very quiet for a while except for the scrunch of the ice when we moved to another position. Chomp, chomp, chomp went our jaws. Colored ice ran down our faces, our fingers, our arms and just naturally ended on our clothes. We didn't pay much attention to the action of the machine. But it was busy turning out cubes like crazy. When Sal had flown in, we just naturally left the door open and so the cubes were naturally moving farther and farther out into the hall like a slow moving glacier. About then I heard the door open. "Hey, that must be Sam," I said to Sal.

Only it wasn't. It was the maid, come to clean up the room. She was carrying an armload of sheets and towels so, of course, she wasn't watching her feet. When she stepped on the first batch of ice cubes she did the neatest dance you've ever seen, trying to get her balance. Only her mad dance took her out onto deeper ice cubes. And then the action got fantastic. She was waving her arms, swiveling her hips, kicking her feet with unbelievable speed. The towels and sheets flew across the room. She jiggled, she jumped. But she couldn't get her balance. Down she went with a jar on those cubes. Bet it was about as comfortable as a fall on a kid's building blocks. Besides, they were chilly. Sal and I stood there staring. Not knowing what we should do. And what happens? The woman gets a glimpse of us and begins screaming. Not little, lady-like screams but full-blown ones. You'd thought she was trying to win an air-raid siren competition.

Now I may not be much to look at. But heck! I'm not used to that kind of reaction. Then I got this glimpse of myself in the mirror. I was streaked with red and blue until I looked like a monster from another world. And Sal wasn't one whit better than me. I did the only proper thing. I stepped toward the maid. And stepping wasn't easy. I meant to give her a hand. Only she wasn't having any help from me. She crawled away from me, panicked. When she got as far as she could go, against the wall, she pulled herself to her feet and had just made one little step toward the door, when I heard Sam's familiar voice. "Tut, tut, tut. What's going on here?"

He didn't get any answer from the maid. Because she let out one little squeak and was gone. I don't mean she vanished. I mean she fainted. Well, wouldn't you, if you saw a red-bearded giant stride smack through a solid wall? I shook my head at Sam. And he grinned, a little apologetically. "I keep forgetting, Tryg," he said, "how much people persons worship the

usual. I just can't remember to use doors when walking through walls is so handy. Open the door, will you, Tryg?"

Which I did. Sam lifted the maid off the floor and carried her down the hall to the supply room to recover. "Less of a shock to come to in familiar surroundings," said Sam.

I wasn't sure of his logic. But I didn't argue. I was too busy eating a grape ice cube. "Now," said Sam when he returned, "what IS going on here?"

"You fixed the ice machine," said Sal.

"So I did. So I did. Remarkable things these ice machines."

"This one is the greatest," I said. "What fllavvvv-vvorrs! Grrrrrreatttttt."

My words come out with these crazy clicky, clacky sounds because I was freezing. Topside, bottomside, inside, outside. I was chilled. My teeth were going like a Spanish dancer's castanets. Holy cow! That bathroom was cold. I kept on eating.

Sam looked about for a moment, puzzled-like. Then he got this absolutely marvelous expression on his face, like a thousand happy thoughts had bubbled up in his brain. "That's it!" he said. "That's it."

"Who's it?" asked Sal. "Are we going to play a game?"

"No, no," said Sam. "No games. Not now. Don't you see? We can sell these. You children need money. Here it is. I told you that something would turn up."

"Sell them?" Sal and I said the same words at the same moment. Like a chorus. Then we said them over again because the idea hadn't sunk into our think place. "Sell them?"

"But how?" I asked. "People won't want to hold them in their hands. The cubes would freeze them and dye them besides. They're too messy."

"True. True. But there has to be a way."

"I know. I know. I KNOW!" shrieked Sal. Since meeting Sam, Sal had not only taken up talking. She'd taken up shrieking whenever she got excited. And with Sam that was fairly often. "Shish-kebabs. We'll fix them like shish-kebabs, on those metal things."

"Very bright. Very bright," I said. "You've forgotten one little point. How are we going to get a hole through the cubes?"

And right then Sam snapped his fingers. "She's got it. I think she's got it. We'll put three on a stick, plastic straws would work as the sticks."

"But the holes, Sam." It's tough being with such impractical dreamers. "We've got to make holes in the ice cubes, Sam."

"But, of course," said Sam. "No problem there. I took away the light beam from my apprentice. He's untrustworthy. We'll use that laser beam to make the holes. It should work swift and neat."

"A lazy beam? Will a lazy beam work?" Sal couldn't understand Sam's words.

And I was thinking, laser beams? Galloping guppies! Fairyland really had gone modern. Or had they had them all the time and we're just catching up? Sal kept repeating her question. "Will a lazy beam work?"

"Laser, laser," I said. "And you'd better believe it! If Sam misses, he might put a hole right through you."

Sal stuck her tongue out at me. She didn't believe my threat. And Sam wasn't listening at all. He was thinking. The more he thought about the plan the better he liked it. In the next moment, Sam became all business. First he asked Sal for money. And that little rat had some too. Here we'd been on short funds and she'd never mentioned her hoard. Sam pocketed Sal's few dollars and said he'd go off and buy the plastic drinking straws and some large plastic bags. He told Sal and me to get six big metal wastebaskets. "The ones in the supply room would be fine," he said. "Also, shovel all the cubes into the tub. They can melt there without damaging anything. We'll have to start with fresh ones. I doubt if people want to eat stuff you've been tramping over."

He had a point there. Before I could ask what we should use for shovels, Sam was gone. Sal was already moving toward the door to go after the wastebaskets. So what could I do, but follow. Looked like we were about to go into business again.

11

Something Always Turns Up

We WERE PRETTY busy for the next hour. First off, Sal and I found the wastebaskets exactly where Sam had said they would be. We had to step over the maid who was still stretched out flat on the floor. I felt her forehead and listened for her breathing. She was alive, so I let her lie there. I thought she'd take a dim view of any request by Sal and me, so we quietly picked up the wastebaskets and left. After all, we were only going to borrow them for a while.

Back in the room, Sal and I found we could scoop up the ice cubes with the baskets. I wedged the door shut on the ice machine. And that stopped production. Because otherwise that mad machine was making them almost as fast as we were getting rid of them. Sal dumped basket after basket of cubes into the toilet and flushed them away. And I ran boiling water onto the piles I was dumping in the tub. Pretty soon we were actually down to the tile floor. It was work. But a fun kind of work. And finally we managed to get the floor in decent shape before Sam came back.

If we'd been busy before, we found we could be

even busier. Sam had us jumping around like we had
Mexican jumping beans in our feet. First, we watched
as Sam lined the washbasin with plastic. Next, he
made a slide from the ice machine straight into the
basin. While he was working at this, Sal and I lined
the metal baskets with large plastic sacks. And then
we set up an assembly line. We couldn't see that light
beam, but Sam had to be holding something, because
whenever he held an ice cube up to his hand, this neat
hole appeared. And the hole went all the way through
too. Well, Sam was the hole-maker and Sal and I were
the sticker-oners. We put three or four colored ice
cubes on each plastic drinking straw. Frit-frat! They
were pretty. Why they looked good enough to eat, if
you know what I mean.

We got those wastebaskets filled with colored ice
kebabs in record time, I bet. And next thing we knew,
Sam was leading us toward the elevators, the freight
elevators. Sal had one basket. I was carrying two.
And Sam had three gripped in his arms. I noticed
people gawking at us when we reached the street.
And when I looked at Sal, I knew why. We had forgotten to wash ourselves. We had cleaned the floor
and clean forgotten our faces and arms. With our red,
white and blue smudges decorating almost every part
of us, we were crowd stoppers. That's for sure.

Sam led us up to the corner near the hotel where a
huge new building was going up. People had to walk
along a wooden walkway built in the street. But
right at the curb was a cleared out spot where the con-

tractor stored supplies. There was a bit of empty space behind some piles of lumber. We climbed in there, put our baskets on the lumber and were ready for business. Only who would ever know that freaks like us had stuff to sell — cooling, delicious, fruity, frosty ice cubes for sale. I almost got carried away with my own long-winded thoughts.

But before I could put my question into words, Sam began shouting. And when Sam shouted, people persons couldn't ignore him. He commanded attention like a hurricane at full force. Besides, with red beard bristling, his little fringe of red hair glowing like a halo, his crazy out-of-this-world clothes, he was something to look at too. People stopped and gawked. And listened too. Sam was shouting, "FRUIT-ICE-KE-BABS — TRY THAT NEW SENSATION — FRESH ICE-KEBABS." He held two or three in each hand like tinker toys on a stick. But I thought they looked delicious, in all their frosty red, white and blue.

"Two bits — a quarter. Try something new," shouted Sam.

And people did. By the dozens. Sam collected the money and Sal and I dipped into the wastebasket to get the ice-kebabs. We got so busy that we were working away like mechanical whirling dolls. Dipping down and reaching out, dipping down and reaching out. It's sure true that you can't keep a good thing secret. Course it was terribly, awfully hot. And those ice cubes were refreshing. People began coming back for seconds and thirds. Business was great and get-

ting greater. We got to the end of the first basket and the second and the third and the fourth and finally the fifth. But the sixth basket seemed bottomless. The longer we worked the tireder Sal and I got. It felt like the afternoon was going on forever.

I stopped to wipe the sweat off my forehead. And right away somebody was hollering to "hurry it up." I got a glimpse of a uniform, a dark uniform way at the back of the crowd. And I heard a voice, a very official voice saying, "Let me through here. Come on, folks, let me through."

But nobody was willing to give an inch. A little thought flickered in my brain and then sprang to life. "Hey, Sam," I said.

Sam kept right on making change beside me. "Sam, do we have a license or something useful like that?"

"Botheration and bubble gum!" said Sam. "I keep forgetting all this people person red tape."

He began rubbing the wen on the end of his nose and I got a relieved feeling. Any moment now he'd find a license right there in his pocket. But that crazy godfather! he wasn't materializing a license. He was shrinking. Right there in front of everyone he began to get smaller and smaller. The other people didn't seem to notice, but I could sure tell what was happening. Sam didn't let his changing size bother him. He kept right on working. He went from six feet, to five feet, to four.

"Sam, Sam, watch it! What are you doing, Sam?"

I yelled this right in his ear. Which was easy because his ear and my mouth were at the same level.

I could hear the policeman. He was getting closer. But even though he kept demanding to be let through, people wouldn't budge. Not much. Those in the front row kept urging us kids to hurry with their ice-kebabs and at the same time were snarling at those

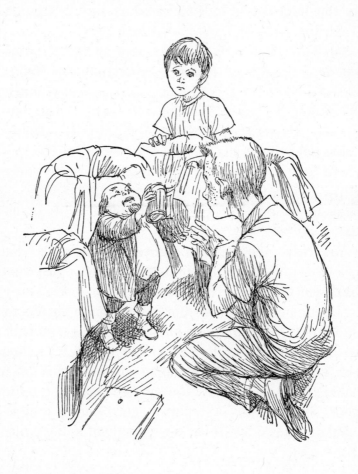

behind to quit shoving. So Sal and I kept handing out those crazy sticks and Sam kept taking money, shrinking smaller and smaller. Suddenly, I looked at him again. What a jolt! Sam was only eighteen inches high. "The money, Tryg, the money," said Sam.

His voice was still big even though he was only knee-high. I dropped down beside him. Sam held out this huge roll of bills and a whole sack of change. "Take the money, Tryg. Good luck, boy."

Sal flung herself down screaming at Sam to wait. But Sam was gone. People in the front row hadn't missed a bit of the action. They were shrieking things at one another like, "Did you see that?" "The man was ice. He melted." "Melted?" "Yeah, he melted." Crazy wild things like that. I sat looking at the spot where Sam had been and I thought I heard his voice, wispy as if he were far away, saying, "Shortage of magic in my land, you know. Hard times there. Good-bye, good-bye."

And that's the way the policeman found us. Sal sprawled out on the ground touching the last spot she'd seen Sam and sobbing her heart out. Me kneeling beside her, dazed-like, but holding on to the money as ordered. Of course, you know what happened next. Sal and I got hauled off to the police station for selling stuff without a license. I suppose if we hadn't been making so much money, they would have told us to scoot. But big business always gets you in trouble.

Sal never said a word as we rode along in the police

car. And it was a strange silence. The old kind of silence. I had an awful feeling that she was retreating into her no-talking world again. And that troubled me. I almost called her Solveig, because the old Solveig was back. Course, I wasn't any picture of joy myself. "Sam is lost, the folks are lost, you are lost too." That was the refrain beating through my mind. I felt drained of energy. I couldn't even get my brain to shift gears into a different thought. I kept on with the same one . . . lost . . . lost . . . lost.

And then Sal spoke. What she said was so absolutely right that my hopes sprang right back to life. Sal said, "Don't worry, Tryg. Something will turn up." And darned if she didn't give my hand a comforting squeeze. She was some kid!

I grinned at her. And she smiled back, very weakly. But somehow it made us both feel better. First off at the station they wanted to know our names. Sal, her short hair wildly flying, looked like a real gone pixie. Especially with those red and blue streaks all over her. She grabbed my hand tight and said nothing. I kept my mouth clammed shut. Because I was suddenly afraid. I knew how furious my dad would be to find Sal and me involved with the police. He took a dim view of breaking the law. I guess as a lawyer he had to. Somehow I had to figure a way out of this mess.

"Come, come, children. Cat got your tongues?" said a squarish policeman. "You must have names."

"Sal," said my sister.

"Sal," said the officer writing it down. "What comes after Sal?"

I was desperately trying to signal Sal to keep quiet. But once underway, Sal was impossible to shut off. "Samsen," she said in clear tones. And then burst into loud wails. Just saying our name made her think of Sam.

The officer wrote it down, careful like. But what happened next didn't make sense. Because he began hollering. Absolutely hollering as if he were having some kind of fit. I grabbed hold of Sal and hid her face against my shirt, and covered her ears with my hands. That policeman had gone crazy. He was yelling for Corcoran, for Daly, for Jones. And at the same time he was grabbing at the papers on his desk hunting something. He finally latched on to a picture. I could tell from the shape. He kept waving it in my direction, but I couldn't focus on what the picture was about. I had this sinking sensation that maybe he had recognized us as the kids with the kooky Admiral or maybe the ones who had gone down with the seats.

Other policemen were racing in. Reporters joined the mob. And they all seemed to be shouting. Somebody grabbed my hand and started shaking it. Others were yelling to nobody in particular. "It's them. Hey, Mulligan found the two kids — the kidnapped kids." "Where's the red-beard?" yelled someone else. Words, words, words. I felt like a million words were bombarding my numb ears.

But if we thought those moments were wild we only had to wait a minute for everything to get crazier yet. Good thing that those adventures with Sam had put us in shape to accept the ridiculous as normal. The crowd became a mob. And we were the center of it, shoved this way, pulled that. People hollering questions. Flashbulbs going off. People hugging us and each other. Then Mom seemed to materialize out of the crowd with Dad right behind her. Mom looked awful, like she'd been putting in full time at crying. And Dad didn't look much better. Like maybe he'd been on his feet a million hours. Strangely though, they both looked awfully happy. Which was odd considering that Sal and I looked like red, white, and blue globs. Dad hugged me and Mom kissed Sal and started crying. And then Dad was shaking my hand until I thought he was going to pump it off my body.

Mom kept saying, "My babies, my babies."

There's a nauseating statement. I haven't been a baby for a long time. And my dad, my dad who is about the best lawyer ever to hit a courtroom and can spill out words that hold you spellbound, my dad couldn't seem to get any words out at all.

But I finally did find out what all the hullabaloo was about. Remember those kids that were kidnapped? Galloping guppies! Those kids turned out to be us. Sam's apprentice had lost Mom and Dad because they were put on an emergency flight back to the United States, all because Sal and I had vanished at Kennedy

Airport. My cablegram had messed everything up, mainly because Mom and Dad had never heard of any Sam and when we seemed swallowed up in New York, the police assumed we were kidnapped. I guess they had every police force in every state in on the act. People kept reporting they had seen us in spots like Miami Beach, Kankakee, Los Angeles, and Butte. Even with Sam's magic we would have had a rough time making all those places. Of course, with Sal's hair cut in that new pixie style, the way she looked now and the way she looked in the published pictures had little resemblance to one another. No wonder we were never recognized.

While all the exclaiming was going on I had one of those sudden hunches. Pretty soon somebody was going to pop the big question. "Where HAD we been?" Now how much should I tell? As Sam had warned us often enough, people persons worshiped the usual — they detested the unusual. I decided to start with the usual. So I told the whole group how we'd been with our godfather, Sam.

Hardly were those words out when another shouting match began. Dad was shouting that we didn't have a godfather, not one named Sam or anything else. The police were yelling things like "See? See?" at whoever would listen, because they'd been having a hard time convincing reporters that there really was a red-bearded Sam. The reporters were yelling questions about who Sam really was.

I should have known better. It's always easier to

get into a tight situation than out. Once I'd admitted that we had been with Sam I was trapped. I had to go on. Sal suddenly lifted her head from my dad's shoulder where she was resting it. "He was nice. Sam was about the nicest thing ever," said Sal.

"Yes. Yes, he was," I put this in quickly. "His name was Sam Bottleby." Oh, oh, here we went again.

"What an odd name," said my mother. And the reporters raised a murmur of sound as they commented.

I went on doggedly. "He took us to the New York Manor House."

"Expensive taste, I'd say," said my dad. "Go on, go on. What then? Did he tie you up? Beat you?" I guess we did look a little beat.

"That's all," I said. "That's absolutely all."

"That's ALL?" There were disbelieving shouts from all over the room. They were expecting some kind of horror tale. People sure do like horror dished out in great bloody gobs. "Well, we had room service for our meals," I said. "Sam said he'd let us know when you arrived. He must have forgotten." I said that lamely.

"FORGOT!" That set off another screaming match as each person tried to tell someone else just why that villain of a Sam had forgotten. It was awful. Because they were saying terrible things about Sam. And here he had been so nice.

"Sam took us to Central Park and on a ferry ride and

down in a subway. And we saw the Mets play with
balls that weren't there and . . . and . . ." Sal
stopped. Finally she had gotten my signal to shut
up.

Then Mom started in, all excited. "She's talking.
Solveig's talking. Did you hear her, Daddy? She's
really talking."

Come to think of it Sal had said more words in
those moments than Mom and Dad had heard in the
last year from her. I'd gotten sort of used to her chat-
ter by now.

"Sam called me Sal. That's my name now. I want
to be called Sal."

"We'll see about that," said my father in his very
familiar no-nonsense tone.

"If it matters to the child, please let's not quibble,
dear," said Mother. "But oh, your beautiful hair. What
happened to your beautiful hair?"

"Tryg cut it," said Sal. Now that was a big help.

"Trygve," Mother looked aghast.

I was in for it, obviously. But I started talking
like mad, hoping I could explain. "We couldn't keep
Sal's hair looking decent, Mom. It looked awful,
all the time. So we cut it off."

I was going to let the whole thing drop. But Sal
had to volunteer more.

"Sam sold it," she said.

"Enterprising devil," said my father. "Trying for
every cent, wasn't he?"

Sal and I were very sure not to say exactly how

much Sam had gotten for the hair. I knew we'd really be in deep water if we should mention that. "We needed money for the hotel bill, Dad," I said.

"He sold Sal's hair to pay your bills? At the Manor House? You've got to be kidding," said my father. "He couldn't have even gotten a good start on a hotel bill with what he could get for Sal's hair."

I didn't argue. I retreated. "Sam said he got a lot of money," I said, implying that maybe he had added his own money to ours.

"He was awfully nice," said Sal. The adults gathered around still looked very doubtful.

Then Dad spotted the roll of bills in my one hand and the sack of change. "Where did you get all this money?" asked Dad. He took the bills from me and I was suddenly aware of how awfully much was there. Maybe hundreds of dollars. I swallowed. I couldn't find much volume for my words. "We sold ice-kebabs," I said.

"You sold what?" Everyone was shouting the same question. I had to repeat my answer. "Ice-kebabs," I said, firmly, this time. "They were ice cubes on a stick — like shish-kebabs."

"Sam made them for us right in our bathroom ice machine," said Sal. "They had lovely flavors — cherry and lemon-pineapple and grape. U'mmmm." A happy smile flitted over her face as she thought of the tastes.

The expressions that greeted our explanations were wild. Never have I seen a bunch of more confused grown-ups. They couldn't figure out whether we were the world's greatest liars, slightly balmy or maybe dopey with drugs. Then before any more questions were popped, I said, "I'm so tired, Dad. I bet Sal's tired too. Could we have dinner, please?"

That threw Dad into forward gear. He said very firmly to the police and reporters that questioning would have to wait. Everyone was exhausted. He was right about that, all right. I felt drained of everything, just a great hulk of nothingness at the moment. Dad expected agreement and he got it. All of us started outside, Dad carrying Sal and Mom hanging on to me as if she were afraid I'd disappear. As we came outside I noticed this little old man going by. I wouldn't have looked twice except for that crazy fringe of red hair around his bald top. Sal's hand reached down and gripped my shoulder. Sal had seen him too.

The old man shuffled by us and he said in a scratchy nasal voice, not at all like Sam's, but the words were the same. He said, "If you're going to have an adventure make it first class. And always, always enjoy it." Those were all the words, but a funny sound like a chuckle followed after.

As we were getting into the car we heard, very faintly, the words . . . "Something will turn up. You'll see . . ."

"Good-bye, Sam. Good-bye," called Sal.

And in my brain I echoed Sal's words. "Good-bye, Sam, good-bye."

"What's that? What's that?" asked Dad. "Is he here. Is that man here?"

But Sam was gone. I guess he had only come to say good-bye. And inside I felt a twinge of sadness. With the rationing of magic in fairyland, we might never see Sam again. Still, we had had a first-class adventure. And maybe, just maybe something would turn up. We could always hope that the something turning up would be Sam, good old Sam Bottleby, godfather first class.